Sojourner

Marguerite Antonio

SOJOURNER

Published by Marguerite Antonio , Edmonton, Canada

Cover artwork by Richard Lotnick

ISBN:
Paperback 978-1-77354-461-8
ebook 978-1-77354-462-5

Publication assistance by

Acknowledgements

The researching for and writing of a novel can be
a solitary process but it is one I enjoy.
Getting the novel ready for the readers is, however,
one that requires many caring and talented others.
Sincere thanks to:
Karen Moore for her many hours of critiquing and editing
Dorothy Sera for her loving encouragement and input
Richard Lotnick whose painting inspired the cover design
Dale Youngman and the caring and talented staff at
PageMaster Publishing.
And
To you, the reader, thank you for choosing this book.
Enjoy.

Chapter 1

He awoke with a start, his heart pounding in his chest. Etroygylus lay perfectly still on the pallet in his sleeping chamber, his senses on full alert, trying to discover what had awoken him. Silence greeted him, and he didn't feel anyone else in the room. Slowly he opened his eyes to the darkened chamber even as the ambient light in the room brightened gradually; there was nothing to explain his sudden jolt from slumber.

His heart rate slowly returned to normal. Then he heard a distant thud, felt a slight tremor, and heard a muffled screech. 'Ah,' Etroygylus thought, 'more turbulence is all.'

He rose and padded softly to the elimination and cleansing chamber where he efficiently performed his morning ablutions. Then, as he did every day, he switched on the holographic image of his human model, Kevin Warden. Examining his own naked body carefully, he smiled and turned to face the image.

"Hi there. Yes, we could be brothers or cousins, don't you think? Or I could be your grandson. And I must remember to think of myself as Troy Gilles, not Etroygylus. I hope we can meet someday my friend, but this voyage is taking longer than we first anticipated," he said.

Another muffled thud reminded Troy that he needed to get moving. 364C, his robot/valet/personal assistant, had placed a pressurized body suit on the bed and a breakfast tray on the small table nearby.

"Troy, you are to be present on B deck at 0800 hours," the smaller rotund robot reminded him.

"Thank-you Cee, I'll be there," Troy replied. "What have we to eat this morning?" he asked after donning the suit and sitting down to his morning meal.

"It is called porridge, I believe," Cee replied stiffly, or as stiffly as a mechanical device could.

Troy laughed. Since he had programmed it so, Cee did have a way of mimicking the accent and behaviour of the ancient English butler they had read about in their Earth history studies. Troy tasted the porridge. 'Hmm, not that bad,' he thought.

Here on E deck the crew was required to learn to eat and assimilate food like that which earth humans consumed so their bodies would adapt. They would not be able to rely on the nutritional pellets and capsules which nourished the others on this great Mothership Xernex. E Deck was engineered to simulate gravity and other aspects of Earth's ambience. It had its own air-filtrations system and grew the food in hydroponic chambers. All this and more was done to help the hand-picked young crew to acclimatize to planet Earth. Troy was proud to have been selected to be part of this mission.

Elyngtren, or Ellen Trent, another member of the Earth mission crew popped into his chamber as he finished his meal. She scrunched up her face in disgust. "Yuck, that porridge stuff is awful!" she exclaimed, "but I guess we'd best get used to it. Are you coming?"

"It wasn't so bad, Ellen, and we will be eating worse by the time we get there, I'm sure," Troy replied as he rose to join her. "Let's get to B deck and see what's happening. Did those tremors and noises awaken you this morning, as well?"

"Yes, what do you think it was?"

"Turbulence? I wonder if we made it into Earth's orbit last night?" he asked, his eyes alight with anticipation.

Ellen's expression echoed his own delight. Like Troy, Ellen had also been hand picked for this mission. This assignment to go to Earth was a dream come true for her, and though she had been on short intergalactic flights before, this was an especially important mission because it would be her last one. She and Gresylon, her bespoken partner, would be settling on Fentanys, their home planet, to start a family after she returned.

"You heard from Gresylon recently?" Troy asked with a teasing grin.

"Oh yes, we spoke last night," she replied with a wistful sigh. "He has procured an abode for us in our own home center that will be perfect for raising a family. Of course, he is very excited and happy for me about being chosen for this mission."

Troy gave her a light punch on the arm. "Well, let's get on with it then. You've a job to do first."

"Well then, you better *get with it*, yes?" she replied with a cheeky grin, practicing the use of an old human English expression.

Troy smiled and together they passed through the portal to D deck, then joining others, they wafted up to B deck. On

E deck, they were held down by the simulated gravity, and did not require the pressurized space-travel suits; but above that level gravity was not an issue, so they moved from one place to another easily. An Aide met the group at the entrance to the conference chamber.

"Find your seats and strap in," he commanded briskly, "Ebenverious will join you shortly."

The group eyed one another nervously. Ebenverious (Ben to his family and friends) was the Mothership's Commander-in-Chief. The crew members rarely saw the man. They were taught and trained by others under his command. Even Troy, who was Ben's natural nephew, seldom saw him other than at rare family gatherings.

Troy studied the others, fifteen in all. Would Uncle Ben be pleased with them, with their progress? Ben was a powerful man, both physically and intellectually. He exerted strong influence here on Mothership Xernex. Fair skinned with dark brown silver-streaked hair and piercing blue eyes, he was taller than Troy by several inches, and he had an air of command that intimidated most people. Ebenverious was not a man to trifle with, Troy knew. Though he was slightly shorter in stature and had been genetically adapted to resemble earth humans, Troy still resembled Ben physically, and he respected him greatly, trying hard to emulate his uncle in all ways.

Troy's mission-mates were a mixed group: men and women, dark skinned and light, aged between early twenties and late forties in Earth years. All members were specifically chosen, honed, and adapted for their unique duties and capabilities. Their mission was one of reconnaissance - to infiltrate the human communities on Earth in order to study, observe and report on the conditions there. A cry had been sent forth to the Intergalactic High Counsel regarding the serious pollution problems on Earth. Xernex had been dispatched to study this problem and to help formulate solutions.

Four three-person teams would land simultaneously at four different locations on the planet for this purpose. The other three members were trained as extras and could take over the job of any of the others if needed, but they would mainly remain on Xernex as communications assistants to the landing parties.

This mission was quite an undertaking, but as Troy knew, other non-Earth beings had done this in the past. Glancing around the room, Troy could feel the anxiety and anticipation of his teammates as Ebenverious entered and took his seat.

"Good day," the Commander-in-Chief greeted, using a well modulated speaking voice. He spoke in Common; a language that resembled the ancient Aramaic of Earth and was the main dialect spoken in this sector of the galaxies for travel and commerce. It was also the language of Troy's home planet, Fentanys. Each team member was tutored in the Earth's English language as well as the language and dialects of the area into which they would infiltrate.

The crew sat up straight at attention. "I have been briefed on and am happy with your progress," the commander added, putting them at ease. "As you may have noticed, we are experiencing some turbulence; it is caused by a bombardment of space debris that has punctured portions of the outer plasmodial shell of Xernex. I share this with you because we will need to slow our progress somewhat while the outer shell repairs itself. This will mean a delay in the timeline for your evacuation to the planet Earth. Do you have any questions?"

"How serious are the tears in the shell, Sir?" Raj asked. Raj was the eldest of the group at forty-two earth years. He and his team would be landing in the Arabian desert to infiltrate the Arab communities there.

"We have sustained a significant breach to the left anterior wall and several other tears as well. These are repairable, but it will take time. We have now passed by the debris, but as I said, it will take time to heal, thus delaying your mission."

"How close are we to Earth's orbit?" asked the dark-skinned Maria, whose team would be landing in the centre of the African continent.

"Close," Ben answered with a smile. "As your instructor's would have told you, Xernex received permission from Ra to enter this solar system some time ago and we have made good progress since. Our flight path may change because of this delay. Additionally, our forward reconnaissance team has reported major debris (space junk as it is called) in Earth's own orbit. This may mean Xernex will not be able to orbit as closely as we had hoped. We are awaiting more information on that. Then decisions will be made as to when and how we approach the planet. I am sure, however, that you will all be able to navigate your landing modules around this debris."

"Sir, have the forward recon team sighted any hostile actions from Earth beings toward us?" asked Ling. Her oriental features should blend in well as her destination was the South China Sea.

"None as far as we can tell," Ben replied, again with a smile. "Ours is a peaceful mission, a reconnaissance only. Mother Earth knows this. As you know, She and Her flora and fauna will recognize your signature color and auric vibrations and will accept you as a non-threatening guest. How the human population will react we don't yet know. Your job is to blend in, so they do not feel threatened, understood? If there are no more questions, you are dismissed to go on with your day."

"Etroygylus, please meet me in my private lounge," Ebenverious called to Troy telepathically. Troy caught his uncle's eye and nodded.

"I'll meet you guys in the gym later," Troy said to Raj and the others then turned toward the private area. The others smiled knowingly and a bit apprehensively. They all know Troy and the Commander-in-Chief are related. However, Troy never took advantage of that fact and worked as hard or harder than the rest of the crew. Like many of his teammates, Troy had been molded to perform missions like this from an early age.

***

"Uncle Ben, you called?" Troy said and smiled, reaching out to shake his hand. His uncle took his hand and pulled him into a bear hug like he had when Troy was a child, and it felt good. Uncle Ben was a powerful man with a stern manner, but he could be warm and loving as well.

"Here, sit and relax. I called you here for two reasons, son," he began, "but first, have a nutritional pellet and a glass of water before we start. I know you have physical practice after lunch, so you can join me for a moment now."

Ben studied Troy carefully as they chewed and swallowed their quick meal. "I have received intelligence from Fentanys," he said carefully. "Your father's ship has apparently - for lack of a better explanation - gone missing."

"How can that be?" Troy asked, more puzzled than concerned at this point. Troy knew his father was the captain of a fighter ship, the Triton, but the peoples of Fentanys seldom engaged in combat these days.

"It does seem strange. Chestrygus and his crew were dispatched to Ophius, one of the planets in the outer regions of the Sirius star system, to mediate between two opposing factions there. Though prepared for battle, if necessary, Ches was quite confident they could settle the issue peacefully."

"Father has always been a tactful diplomat from what I remember, so what happened?"

"We are not sure. Fentanys has lost contact with his ship, and no debris has been sighted that would indicate an accident or some such. Headquarters isn't even sure if he landed on Ophius."

"Oh," Troy comment, not sure what he was to think of this. He had not seen his father since shortly after his mother had died when Troy was 10 earth years old. His parents had already agreed to have him fostered into the space program, so after his mother's death Troy joined the academy. His father kept in touch, but it was really Uncle Ben who had been his father-image and mentor. "Has anyone tried to contact father telepathically?" he asked then.

Ben laughed, "You know Ches, he never did like 'someone getting into his head'. No, he has either shut down, is ignoring communication, or is unable to communicate. Headquarters is not too worried yet but felt you and I should be aware. There is nothing we can do from here anyway, OK?"

Troy nodded and said quietly, "Yes, thank you for letting me know."

Ben sat studying his young nephew carefully, then nodded as well. "Now, I would like your personal insight into the readiness of members of this mission. I've received all the data from your teachers and trainers but would appreciate your insight, Troy."

Troy sat up straighter. "What would you like to know?" he asked carefully.

His Uncle smiled and said, "Nothing that would make you feel like you are tattling on the crew. No, you have lived and worked with most of the crew for the last 5 years. You know what is required of everyone in this mission. I would like your personal assessment of the other group leaders."

In Troy's opinion, all three were well-adapted for their position so he shared this thought with his uncle.

His Uncle nodded, "Yes, just as I thought. Did your trainers mention our decision to include the personal robots of each group leader on the landing module?"

"No! Syvers hasn't mentioned that to us yet, but I think it is a fine idea, sir. Cee, that is 364C, is very adept at communication, a good help in an emergency and has been working in the module with me often enough to understand the basics."

Ben nodded and said, "Yes, so we have observed. Troy, it was your work with Cee, as you call the robot, which led us to consider programming the personal robots of the other group leaders accordingly. We feel the robots could remain on the module after landing and assist with communications and such."

Troy's eyes sparkled and he grinned at his uncle saying, "Well, I'd better not crash the module in the ocean then. We wouldn't want Cee to rust!"

Ben chuckled, then grew serious again. "It will be your job to assist the other three in training their personal robots as well. Can you handle that?"

"Yes, if Maria's, Raj's, and Ling's robots are as adept as Cee, it will be fun."

"Good," Ben said with a smile. Then studying his nephew carefully again, he added, "Troy, one of your many skills lies in your profound ability in mental telepathy, does it not?"

"Yes, I have been able to communicate that way since before my mother died. It was she who taught me the skill and honed my efforts, as you know," Troy replied.

"Troy, do you think you could try to contact Ches?" Ben asked.

Troy thought about this. Depending on the situation, trying to contact his father telepathically could be dangerous to his father, and to Xernex as well, if hostile units managed to infringe on their conversation. There were several factions within the Intergalactic Council who had opposed their mission to earth even though the majority ruled in favor. Also, his father had been sent to intermediate in a dispute that could put him in a perilous situation as well.

Ben seemed to understand Troy's hesitation. "You know how to protect your conversation, Troy," he reminded him, "and you have been honing that skill even more carefully since your mother's tutoring. This is one of your talents that makes you so valuable to the Earth mission. I think it may be one way to determine what has happened to your father now as well. What do you say to giving it a try?"

"Okay, I will try to contact father after our meditations this evening. I'll be more relaxed then and will be able to shield myself and hopefully Father as well."

"You will report directly to me."

"Of course."

Ben smiled and rose from his seat. Troy rose as well, and his uncle gave him another hug. "I am proud of who you have become, Etroygylus, and I am sure Ches will be as well. Now off you go to your lessons, young man."

Troy knew he has been dismissed. His thoughts were churning as he wafted back down to E-deck and changed into his track suit for physical training. As he joined the group, his instructor merely nodded at him, but a few of his mission-mates sent him inquiring glances.

It was Raj who finally asked, "So, the Commander-in-Chief was pleased with our preparation for the mission so far?"

Troy chuckled. "My Uncle asked me to remain mainly because of some family business and yes, it is as he said; he's happy with our progress. Knowing Uncle Ben though, I would suggest we keep up the good work. He keeps a close watch on all of us."

"Troy has that right, and you'd all best remember it as well!" their instructor said, with a nod and smile.

While chatting with his teammates during the evening meal of corn, green vegetables and soy patties, and again later after their evening meditation session, Troy had trouble remaining engaged in the conversation. He felt tense and tried to relax, but thoughts of how to go about safely contacting his father simmered in the back of his mind. He declined the invitation to join a few of the others for a game of three-tiered chess before bedding down for the night. Then he dismissed Cee and sat at his desk.

Troy first said a prayer asking for protection for both him and his father then tried to conjure up a holographic image of his father, but he could not seem to remember his father's facial features clearly. It had been many years since he had seen Chestrygus. He had been much younger then and had undoubtedly changed, as his father would have by now, as well. Troy sat back with a sigh, then staring into the space across his desk, he whispered, "Father...Chestrygus..., can you hear me?" Nothing. Troy sighed then tried again.

"Father...Dad...it is I, Etroygylus, trying to contact you. Can you safely reply please?" Troy spoke aloud. A slight mist seemed to form on the other side of the desk. Speaking in ancient Aramaic, Troy again called upon his angelic guardians for protection as he stared into the mist.

"Father?" The mist swirled slowly and began to form an indistinct image. Troy waited.

"Son," came a weak reply.

Troy sat up straight, peering into the mist opposite.

"Father, where...can you...are you safe?" he blurted.

"As safe as possible, son, and you?" The image wavered but Troy did recognise his father's voice and relaxed.

"We are well, and we send our greetings and good wishes," Troy replied, wondering how much he could ask or share.

"Ah yes, you are with Ben and faring well, I hear. You do me proud, my son, and your mother would have been proud of who you have become as well." After a short silence, Ches continued to speak. "Etroygylus, tell Ben we are safe. We did encounter hostilities prior to orbiting Ophius, we sustained considerable damage, and we were drifting off course. We eventually found and then landed on a smaller planet outside of the known solar systems." Again, there was a pause as though Ches was carefully weighing his words. "This planet has the necessary requirements for rebuilding our ship and to sustain life. The natives are primitive but eager to assist."

"Ah, my father the space explorer," Troy said jokingly. Then he added more seriously, "And its protector."

His father uttered a weak chuckle and said, "We are safe for now. Tell Ben to take care, and you be careful as well, son. Be ever watchful. Things are not always as they seem, even close by." The voice faded then, but as the mist cleared, Troy thought he heard his father tell him they would be in contact soon.

Troy sighed, his eyes stinging with unshed tears, as old memories of his father surfaced. When had he last seen the man? Troy could not remember exactly, but he did vividly recall the time he and his parents, and a few other families, had made a trip to the seashore.

He must have been four or perhaps five in Earth years. His father had very gently taught him to swim in the waters and had introduced the young Troy to aquatic life like sea otters and friendly dolphins. He and the other children had joyfully played with the animals and even tried to communicate with them under the watchful eye of their parents. This was a memory he would always cherish. But as an adult? Sadly, Troy couldn't remember the last time they had had a face-to-face conversation, though he did recall the time Ben had taken him up to Mission Control Center when the Triton lifted off.

What impressed him there was the great respect, and even awe, the ground crew and commanders, and even the Intergalactic Counsel held for Ches and the Triton crew. It was an awesome yet humbling experience for Troy. His father had acknowledged the accolades afforded him with simple thanks and then gone about his duties to the best of his ability.

"Will I be able to live up to that kind of honor and respect?" Troy wondered and had promised himself, then, that he would always do what was honorable and to the best of his ability as well. Ben had become a sort of surrogate father, but Troy longed to know his biological father more intimately.

He sighed again, shook himself, then cast his mind back again to their recent conversation. He realized from his father's words, and from the way he spoke, that all may not be well with him there, or perhaps here on Mothership Xernex too. Rather than using his electronic tablet, Troy searched out a piece of paper and pencil. Relying on his near-photographic memory, he recorded Ches's words and pauses as exactly as he could, then telepathically called his uncle. His uncle responded immediately, telling Troy to meet with him outside the conference room on C deck within five minutes. Troy immediately called for Cee.

A knock, then his door opened, just as Cee finished helping him back into the pressurized suit. Raj entered and eyed Troy quizzically.

"Going for a stroll upstairs at this time of night?"

Why was Raj questioning this? What was he getting at? Or am I just being paranoid? Troy wondered. He shrugged and said, "I just forgot to give something to my uncle."

"What? Can't it wait until morning?" Raj said with a slight sneer. Yes, Raj was curious or wary, Troy decided. He would have to mention this conversation to Ben, Troy thought, but merely patted Cee on the dome and quipped, "you will all find out about this in the morning," pretending this was about the robots being part of their mission. Slipping past Raj, he hurried to the portal and out to C deck.

Ben motioned for Troy to join him in an alcove across the hall. Silently, Troy handed his uncle the notes he had written of his conversation with Ches. The man read it and frowned.

"So, all is not as well as we thought. Did you get the sense of immediate danger to him and the crew?"

"No, I don't think so, but he was being careful, don't you agree? And I did get the impression he was warning you as well regarding our mission and possibly, oh, I don't know, a spy or infiltrator here on Xernex," Troy replied carefully.

"Yes, from this I would assume he has some intelligence we don't, so will need to proceed carefully. Do you think he may contact you?"

"Yes, I think so. How much of this do you share with Fentanys? Maybe I'm being paranoid, but it seems Raj has been extremely interested in this whole matter," Troy said then shared with his uncle what Raj had said and how he had behaved.

Uncle Ben smiled and said, "Troy, that may only be a bit of professional jealousy on his part, you know. You are quite young to be a group leader and you are my nephew as well."

"Yes, but I have worked just as hard or harder than others to attain this position," Troy replied rather cockily.

Ben chuckled, "Yes, so you have. We will keep an eye on your mission-mates. It is not unusual for governments or even enemies to have placed 'sleepers' aboard missions like ours to report back our findings and progress. Usually, we are aware of who these people are and can watch them, but if Ches thinks we may have intruders among us, or that someone at Command Central is passing information to undesirables, we need to know and know quickly. I will pass this information on to our top security team."

"What can I do to help?" Troy asked.

Ben glanced at the younger man thoughtfully and said, "Just go about your daily routine as usual, but report back to me personally should you find anything to be odd. Should your father contact you, be very careful and report to me immediately. Oh, and see if you can get coordinates on this new planet he has discovered. That is rather exciting, don't you think?"

"Yeah, my father the space explorer! Wow! But don't worry, I won't divulge any of this to anyone," he promised seriously.

"I know that, because you will be too busy teaching the other group leaders how to program their robots, right?" Ben said with a grin as he gave Troy one of his bear hugs before turning to go.

Sleep did not come easily to Troy as he thought of all that had occurred and all he had just learned. Helping to teach the others to program their robots would be fun, and the anticipation of the landing on Earth, that wonderous blue-green planet, was huge. And now, what he and Ben had just surmised from his father's comments...well it was a lot to think about. And would his father contact him soon? He hoped so. Troy's mind whirred but eventually calmed, and he fell into a deep sleep.

Chapter 2

Onboard the Mothership Xernex, excitement ran high. They had entered Earth's orbit a few days earlier and had maneuvered into position without incident. Now, after a final briefing, the four crews were loaded into their Landing Crafts, ready to evacuate the mothership to land on Earth. The Commander-in-Chief had come to the departure bay to speak with each captain and crew individually and to change the rotation of descent at the last minute, so Troy would be the last to leave Xernex. Then he gestured for Troy to step aside and spoke with him quietly. This would not have caused speculation, as the crew all know that Troy was the Commander's nephew, but he spoke quietly none-the-less.

"Troy, we have just now received intelligence that Ling may not be what we think she is. Watch her carefully on descent and once on earth. Report to me telepathically if needs be."

"Ling? I would have thought Raj a traitor if we had one," Troy whispered in surprise.

His uncle clasped Troy by the shoulders and smiled. "Just be careful, son," he replied. Then, turning to the crew, he said, "You are all well prepared for this mission - Troy, Ellen, Brad, and you too Cee," he added with a smile. "Go, perform your tasks well. Aid Mother Earth and do Fentanys proud. Good luck and Godspeed."

The departure bay doors slowly opened as the countdown began. Maria left first and quickly attained orbital speed. She kept to her flight path while deftly dodging Earth debris, man-made satellites, and space stations.

Raj followed, equally as adept as Maria.

Ling was next. She whipped her craft to maximum speed, darting and dodging around the obstacles and seemed to be aiming straight for Raj's craft. Troy gasped as he watched. What was happening?

"Raj, to your left," Troy shouted into the communications device, "Ling seems to be out of control of her craft."

Got that," Raj replied and swiftly darted up, then back and behind Ling. There was a sudden flare of light as he did so. "She blazed me!" Raj shouted in astonishment.

"Damage?" Troy asked.

"Not sure, but operational," was the harried reply. "What's she doing? Ling, stop that now. Too dangerous! Get control of your craft!" When he realized that Ling's movements were intentional, he shouted, "Maria, watch your back! She's coming at you!"

"Ling, return to Mothership, now," came the stern command.

A giggle crackled over the intercom. "Not yet. I'm having too much fun!"

"Dead zone, dead zone," came the command, meaning they were not to communicate with open mikes, just one on one with Central Command using personal codes.

"She's going after Maria now," Troy said tersely.

His uncle Ben said, "Troy, the forward guards have her in sight. Go ahead and blast off but stay behind her and remain on your own flight path if you can. Communicate as soon as you can but do not contact the other teams yet. Good luck."

Nervously, Troy gave his crew the go ahead sign and they were off. Like Maria and Raj, he quickly obtained orbital speed and his own flight path. This was utterly amazing! Wow, what a feeling! Silently they circled, descending closer and closer to that beautiful blue green planet, dodging, and weaving around the space junk as they raced toward their destination.

"Wow, this is even more amazing, beautiful, breath-taking than we were taught," Ellen whispered in awe. She released her seat restraints and moved about uncovering all the viewing portals so she could observe their landing visually. Being the craft's navigator, she always saw things via her instrument panel, but she wanted to see this live. "Wow! That beautiful planet. So much. So much water, verdant life, pristine atmosphere. Amazing!"

"Yes, it is," Brad agreed. Troy smiled at them and nodded. He was too busy guiding their Landing Craft and watching for Ling to take the time to talk, but he felt the thrill of it all just like they did.

Troy pointed at the screen. "Look, Maria must have found her entry portal. She has successfully penetrated earth's outer shield. I can't see Raj or Ling."

"Raj, two orbits from penetration, Ling above, surrounded by guards," Cee reported. The crew cheered.

"I knew we brought you along for a reason, Cee, thank you," Troy said with a smile as he slowed the landing craft, dodging around yet another derelict space-station moving into entry orbit.

"Yes, I can see that he will be an asset," Brad started to agree, then gasped and yelled, "Troy, watch your left! Ling has escaped the guards!"

"Damn, what is she up to?" Troy grunted and deftly made a quick, sharp, right-angle turn putting the space station between her and his craft. He scanned the instrument panel, "Where is she?"

"Below, coming up at us…move it, Troy!" Brad yelled.

Troy concentrated fully as he maneuvered the craft in yet another series of sharp turns to fly above the station. Ling followed. Where to now? Troy thought nervously.

Suddenly, he spied another piece of debris ahead, even as the guards were again closing in on Ling. After another sharp right turn, he was above her again, racing toward his entry portal. Tensely, Troy flew in a zigzag pattern, even as he dodged other debris while keeping a close tab on Ling's craft.

They heard a muffled snap just as Ellen cried, "There she is again. Ouch! She blazed us!"

Brad yelled out, "The guards have netted her – they've got her now!"

"Damage?" Troy barked tersely, "do we abort?"

Ellen worked hurriedly at her instruments. Brad and Cee surveyed the outer shell.

"Minimal damage," Brad reported, and Cee confirmed that the guards had corralled Ling again and were heading back up to Mothership Xernex.

Troy glanced at Ellen. She nodded.

"I'll make another pass, then let's get ourselves into entry orbit quickly," Troy quipped. "I'm sure we will be safer down there."

"Wow! I hope so. Great maneuvers there Troy," Brad said as he raised his arms up in the air in a joyful gesture.

Ellen grinned in agreement then huddled over the instrument panels to mark the coordinates for their entry to planet Earth. Oh my, she thought, this is it! We are here. Hello Mother Earth.

"Hang on, here we go!" Troy said. With some quivering and shaking and a great blast of heat, their landing craft penetrated the upper strata of Earth's atmosphere. Having to adjust to the Earth's gravitational pull was a challenge. Their craft shuttered and twisted, the plasmodial shell screeched and shimmered, but Troy managed to make the needed adjustments and slowed down even more, just as they had been taught and had practiced so many times.

They seemed to float down in utter silence. The other two grinned and smiled, giving him the sign of approval.

Troy grabbed his communication device, swallowed hard to rid himself of the emotional lump in his throat and reported in, "Entry accomplished."

"Superbly done, congratulations," was the reply from Central Command.

"What of the other teams?" Troy asked.

"Maria and Raj have entered successfully. Ling is being detained on Xernex. We will advise of further information as decisions are made. Prepare for your own landing."

"Affirmative," Troy replied and signed off. He turned to Ellen, "Coordinates? I'm switching to earth navigational devices now."

"We are over the northern pole. Veer south and west," Ellen replied hoarsely, then gave him the exact coordinates for the landing destination which was in the Pacific Ocean off the shores of the country called Canada.

"Any hostiles?" he asked Brad. Now that they were traveling at a much slower speed, their entry would no doubt have been observed on radar and other devices. They had been warned that the humans could fire upon them and had been trained to dodge these attempts to bring them down, and to avoid retaliating wherever possible. This meant they would have to find adequate cover as soon as they touched down. The outer plasmodial layer of their craft would protect to some degree, but they would need to find an underwater cavern or cave in which to hide. Earth experts had assured Troy that there were such structures in the underwater topography of the landing site.

"Nothing threatening so far, but there certainly are a lot of aircraft in the area, so be watchful."

Troy nodded as he veered their craft in a quick left turn to avoid one of these, then continued the coordinated flight path, slowing even more.

"Brace yourselves, we're going in!" Troy warned the crew. He steered a sharp right turn then plunged straight down. Impact was horrendous. Their landing craft hit the water hard, bounced several times, and rolled sideways before coming to a shuddering stop. Vaguely, out of the corner of his eye, he saw Ellen careening into the control panel – she had forgotten to engage her seat restraints in all the excitement. Troy felt something smash into the back of his head, then all went black.

Chapter 3

Kevin Warden lounged back on the deck chair, one bare foot resting on the opposite knee, soft music wafting from the player beside him. He closed his eyes and heaved a long sigh of relief. He woke with a start a few moments later at the sound of a loud splash in the water below the cabin. He sat up and surveyed the waters. Ah, dolphins cavorting in the bay just beyond their dock. Not Ancion's pod, he decided but watched them with a smile as they moved further south.

"Well Ancion, it's taken us longer than I hoped, but we humans are well on our way to finding solutions for getting your waters cleaned up, just as I promised. I'm just sorry it has taken so long, my friend," Kevin said aloud as he stood and walked over to the railing facing the ocean.

"Talking to yourself again, Kevin?" Rachael, his wife, teased as she slipped an arm around his waist and snuggled up close to him.

Kevin smiled down at her as he eased her back into the deck-chair. "No, actually, I was talking to Ancion."

"Oh, Is he out there?" Rachael asked excitedly, moving over to the railing.

"No, there were dolphins but not his pod. But at the conference Fritz and I just attended, the Dutch delegation displayed the prototype for oceanic clean up and it looks viable, Rachael. The Dutch have incorporated a lot of the technology we shared with them. Fritz thinks it will work to clear up those lakes of garbage collecting in the oceans all over the world and possibly within the next five years."

"Wow, Kevin that's great! I can see where you would want to share it with Ancion," Rachael said enthusiastically, "I still remember that first trip to Gillies Bay where you introduced Ancion to us. You promised him then that you would help clean up the oceans, didn't you?"

"Yes, I did," Kevin agreed, then grinned at her mischievously. "And Melisanna, Ancion's mate, asked if you were my mate. I said you would be, but you didn't know it yet. She said I'd chosen well."

"No!" his wife gasped wide-eyed leaning over to punch him gently on the arm. "You made that up."

"No, I didn't. You remember you asked what we were talking about, the dolphins and I?"

"Yes, but…" she sputtered as Kevin grabbed her and twisted her on to his lap.

"No, it's true and Melisanna was right, I have chosen well," Kevin replied then kissed his wife softly. She melted against him just like she had when they were first married 15 years ago.

"Hmmm," Rachael signed, then wriggled on his lap and nipped Kevin's ear lightly. She giggled, then rose and grabbed his arm, "Come on inside; dad and the kids won't be back for hours." Kevin happily allowed himself to be pulled along.

Later that evening, Rachael and Kevin again sat on the deck watching the sunset. Their children, thirteen-year-old Greg and ten-year-old Keira were settled in their rooms, and Rachael's father, John, was ensconced before the TV watching his favorite science show. "Don't you just love this time of night?" Rachael enthused in a hushed tone, "it's like the world is quietly waiting."

"Yes," Kevin agreed. Except for the soft lapping of the waves on the shore all was still. Even the wind had died down to a gentle warm breeze as the sun slowly sank into the far ocean in a final burst of color. Then the night sounds began to make themselves heard; the wind picked up a little and the night creatures began to stir. "It's even more spectacular when you are sailing in open seas."

They sat in comfortable silence, watching.

"Kevin, do you miss being on and in the water? You spend so much time lately in the lab researching ways to get rid of those awful garbage lakes in the oceans, and in negotiations with other countries about the oceanic pollution problems, that you haven't been able to do your work with the dolphins and other ocean creatures. Do you miss that?" Rachael asked.

Kevin laughed. "I don't do the negotiating. Fritz does. I merely show slides that explain the urgency, and the dangers to sea life, and set forth our ideas as to how to combat the problem. Luckily, many other nations are on board now and in pooling our knowledge we are making headway, slowly. It's not been nearly as quickly as I had hoped when I promised Ancion I would try."

Kevin leaned back and stretched his arms over his head. "Yes Rachael, I would love to meet up with Ancion and his pod again and to swim with them, to compare notes on how things are going for them."

"You think you could still speak dolphin-talk?" Rachael teased, "it's been years since you two got together."

"Oh, I think I could still make myself understood," he quipped with a grin. As a young boy Kevin had befriended a dolphin, Ancion, and they had developed a means of communication that had served both well. Their rapport with one another had been a great boon to the research being done at the University of British Columbia at the time, on trying to decode dolphin and whale sounds. This friendship had also provided the impetus that drove Kevin into the world of marine biology and ocean sciences.

"It's dark enough now," Rachael said as she rose and went over to the telescope mounted on the other side of the deck, "I'm going to see what is out there tonight."

While Kevin studied and worked with the oceans of the world, Rachael loved to watch and contemplate the skies. She had taken several courses in astronomy and studied the latest news from outer space. Several years earlier her father, John, had purchased this powerful telescope for her. Now she watched and mapped the stars regularly when they were on holiday here at the cabin on Savory Island.

"Kevin, come see! There is something out there," Rachael called excitedly, breaking onto Kevin's ruminations, "look, you can see it with the naked eye, there just above the horizon west of Vancouver Island, below Sirius. Wow, look at that! It just did a right-angled maneuver. No satellite can do that."

"Yeah, I see that."

Rachael called out, "Dad, come see what's in the sky!"

"John," Kevin rasped loudly, his voice still inaudible beyond a harsh whisper after an accident that had damaged his larynx when he was 10 years old, "come here; I think we have ourselves a UFO."

"Don't tease. It could be, you know!" Rachael cried, as her father and the children rushed out to the deck. "See over there!" Rachael pointed excitedly. "Look, it did it again, a full 90-degree turn. Wow!"

The family watched in silence as the bright light seemed to slash across the sky coming right at them, then swerved sharply and plunged into the ocean west of Vancouver Island with a brilliant flash of blueish green light.

"Dad," Greg asked in a hushed tone, "do you think it was a UFO? Should we report it to the authorities?"

"That was certainly odd behavior for a meteor, satellite, or such, yes. I'm not at all sure what it was, but I do think the Department of Oceans and Science would have observed it since they keep a close watch on things. I'll give the department a call in the morning."

"I wish I'd gotten a picture of that," Rachael moaned, "it happened so fast I didn't think to do so. Anyway, hot chocolate anyone?"

The family followed her inside, still speculating about what they had just seen.

Chapter 4

Kevin sat at the table with his second cup of coffee and smothered his favorite waffles with Canadian maple syrup. John strode in and grabbed a coffee as well.

"Looks like it's going to be a fine day for fishing," he remarked with a contented sigh as he joined his son-in-law.

"Yeah, looks like," Kevin agreed.

"Something bothering you son?" John asked, leaning closer.

Kevin gave himself a mental shake. "No, not really. I'm still wondering about what we saw last night. There was nothing on the internet about it when I checked earlier. Usually, the media is all over this kind of thing. I thought something would have been reported about that strange sighting."

"You're right about that. The media usually makes a big splash of anything that could be construed as a UFO, but folks are plain tired of hearing about the latest doomsday, 'the aliens are invading' rhetoric. Maybe the media moguls have eventually caught on to that fact."

Kevin laughed, "Don't you wish!"

"I'm ferrying Rachael and the kids over to Powell River today, remember? They want to take in some sort of special movie there so will be staying with your folks for the night. Rachael is going shopping and will return by water taxi later. How about we have a day on the water before you head back to work on Monday? You need to relax Kevin. What with the World-Wide Oceanography Conferences you and Fritz attended, and your research work at UBC and at the Aquarium, you are sometimes stretching yourself too thin, young man. You need to relax more; what better way than by being out on the water on a fine day, huh?"

"Rachael has been complaining to you?" Kevin asked with a sardonic grin.

"Well, she is concerned...and rightly so. You do push yourself hard sometimes. That's no bad thing if you balance it with rest and relaxation."

Kevin sighed and said, "Yah, you're right John. I'll check in with Fritz to see if there is anything that needs immediate attention, then we can be on our way. Hey, how about taking scuba gear and doing a bit of diving? You okay with that?"

"Sure am," John replied with a grin.

By mid-afternoon both men had caught their limit in fish and were lazily making their way north-west of Port Hardy. The sun shone bright and warm; a light breeze fluffed up a few white-caps as an occasional gull circled overhead. It was a perfect day to be on the water. Kevin leaned back in the deck chair. How he missed this. John and Rachael were right - he did need to get back to being on the water more, enjoying the simple pleasures the ocean provided.

"Let's anchor close by here and go for a swim," he said to John.

"Sure, how about that little cove up ahead? It looks like a likely spot to lay anchor."

Minutes later, the men joined the sea life in the water, exploring the nearby ridges and rocks. It was exhilarating for Kevin to be in this milieu again. His work was all about the oceans, but he so seldom got to simply enjoy, to be part of the pleasure of a good swim with the fishes and exploring what was beneath the waves. It felt good, right, he thought as they swam deeper, explored further.

John waved then and they both rose to the surface, shucked their scuba gear and sat down to partake in the lunch Rachael had packed for them. A splash nearby caught their attention.

"Ah, dolphins," John commented. "I didn't spot any below, did you?"

"No, they must have just arrived. Look, they're coming closer to the boat. This group isn't afraid of humans. Is it...?"

A loud whistle and chirp interrupted his thoughts," Quiven?"

Kevin chirped and whistled in return, "Ancion?"

A huge dolphin rose high in the water beside the boat, then it twisted and plunged back down.

"John, I think that's my old friend," he stated in awe, watching as the dolphin drew even closer.

"I do believe it is the same dolphin you used to play with as a child. Kevin, do you think you can still communicate? It's been a while."

"Rachael asked the same thing last night. Oh, I think I can make myself understood," he said, walking closer to the edge of the boat clicking, whistling, and chirping.

"Is that you Ancion?"

Click, Click.

"That's a yes…it's him!" Kevin cried. John moved closer.

"Welcome friend," Kevin clicked and chirped, "healthy you are, and your pod?"

Click, click. "You?"

"Rachael and I, well we are. Two offspring we have."

The dolphin grinned widely, arched high then flopped back down again, "Share with Melisanna, I will."

Kevin knew Ancion's mate approved of his choice of wife. She had indicated so a long ago, when Kevin had first introduced Rachael and her parents to the pod. Gazing at his aquatic friend, Kevin had a thought.

In clicks and chirps, Kevin asked, "A strange craft, did such appear in your waters of late?"

The dolphin circled once, then rose again. "Click, Click"-yes.

"A danger it was to your home?"

"Click" - No.

Kevin turned to John and said, "I think whatever we saw yesterday crashed into the ocean near here, but the sea life doesn't seem to be harmed or concerned by it."

"I wonder if the dolphins know what it was, where it landed? Could they describe it? Take us to the crash sight?" John asked. Kevin tried to communicate these questions, but Ancion merely circled nervously, seemingly not understanding.

Kevin thought for moment. "Ancion, in this craft were humans?"

Ancion circled again, then clicked twice.

"The humans, are they safe?"

Again, the dolphin slowly circled; he seemed to be communicating with his pod members. Then, he made a hesitant click... click.

Kevin was puzzled by these responses, and the dolphin circled restlessly as though trying to communicate more. "Ancion, help we can?"

No answer.

"If so, call on me you will. Listen I shall."

"Click, click." Then with a leap, whistle and click, the dolphin moved away to join his pod as they moved on to deeper waters.

"Bye my friend," Kevin cried, "see you again soon?"

"Click, click," echoed in the bay.

John and Kevin quietly watched as the pod disappeared.

"Well, I see you haven't lost your touch with the animals, Kevin," John said in awe.

Kevin glanced at the man, "I wonder what he meant? What was it that crashed, landed, whatever, into the ocean last night? The sea life, dolphins anyway, seemed to know of it."

John shook his head and muttered, "It's a puzzle. But Kevin, just think about this -that animal still recognizes you - can communicate with you after all these years. He respects, trusts, and honors you greatly. I think he would find a way to let you know if you needed to know, don't you think?"

Kevin nodded, stretched and said, "Let's raise anchor and head home. It's been a full day."

"Yes, it has. Rachael will be annoyed to have missed this."

Kevin chuckled, "Yes, she will."

***

Meanwhile, deep in an oceanic trench near to where Kevin and John had been swimming, the space craft teetered precariously on a ledge, swaying in the current.

"Troy, report to Command. You must report to Central Command immediately."

The words and urgency of the tone slowly penetrated the fog. Troy shook his head to clear it. "Ouch, that hurt!" Troy sat up slowly, trying to get his bearings, to understand what was happening as he gingerly explored the knot on his head with a bloody hand.

"Don't touch that," a voice commanded. Troy squinted against the light.

"Cee? What happened?"

"Pieces of the broken console and other tools and debris that were not secured, flew all about this craft. You sustained a bloody but non-life-threatening head wound. Brad has a broken arm which I helped him to reset, and he is stabilized. Ellen has perished; her neck was broken on impact – she was not restrained in her seat. Our craft has settled, precariously, on a ledge. Central Command requests your immediate response," came the terse reply.

"Thank you, Cee," Troy said as he sat up and carefully surveyed the captain's cabin where he sat. Smaller items had been thrown about during the crash landing, but otherwise all seemed in order there. Slowly, he got to his feet and made his way up to the craft's cockpit.

"Where is Brad?" he asked as Cee joined him.

"He is resting in his berth. I checked the ship's interior, and all seems to be in order except for the portion of the command module that Ellen hit. It has been dented but is still functional. I have not yet assessed the exterior."

"Good work, Cee. Let Brad rest a bit longer while I check things out and contact Central. Glad to have you aboard, Cee," Troy said heartily. The robot really was an asset. Feeling more alert now, Troy stumbled toward the washroom to clean up and check his head, which as Cee had said, was bloody but not a serious cut. Then he went about assessing and documenting damage inside the capsule. As Cee had ascertained, damage inside was minimal. A quick check of the outer camera displays showed a few tears in the plasmodial shell but nothing too serious there either. He and Brad would need to visually check that later.

Ellen's body lay on her sleeping pallet. It was obvious she had hit her head and broken her neck on impact, but Troy also observed reddish markings on her left cheek and forehead. Had she been hit when Ling blazed them? She had said nothing at the time and had very effectively navigated their landing. He would have to investigate this more fully later. Troy and Brad would miss her, as would her family and fiancé back on Fentanys. Troy covered the body with a blanket, bowed his head in a silent prayer for her soul's journey home, then he and Cee left the room.

"She would have died instantly, Troy," Brad said quietly as he walked slowly toward them.

"That is a blessing then, but a shame too. She was so excited to be on this trip, so anxious to see earth…to be here."

"I know," Brad agreed sadly.

Taking a deep breath to clear his head, Troy walked over to the command module and reported to Peter, their Liaison Officer.

"We are so sorry to hear of Ellen's demise. We will inform her family, of course. Stabilize your ship and do a reconnaissance. Report back once all is well there."

"Understood," Troy replied briskly, "what of Maria and Raj? Is Ling still going to land on Earth?"

"Maria and Raj have reported in. As for Ling, the Council is still debating," came the stern reply.

Brad and Troy glanced at one another. "Well!" Brad said, "this certain isn't one of Peter's better days."

Troy nodded and said, "How bad is the arm? I think we should suit up and check the outside manually if your up to it, Brad."

"Best take some nourishment and fluids then relax for a moment before venturing out," Cee suggested. The men agreed and did just that.

"Except for the blaze markings outside the viewing portal by Ellen's station, everything looks to be in working order. We can repair that easily, but we will need to move to a more stable site as soon as possible," Brad commented, after they had surveyed the outside damage.

"I agree. Can you scan the topography of this area for a small cavern or such nearby? I felt a warmer current toward the lee of the craft. Did you notice that? There may be an underwater hot pool or geyser nearby that could give you a reference point as to where on Earth we are."

"We have the coordinates Ellen gave you for landing and we can't be far off that, don't you think?" Brad suggested.

"True, but it felt like we bounced and rolled after touchdown so I'm not sure. I'll bring up those coordinates as a starting point."

Both men worked in silence for a time, then Troy said, "Here Brad, see this? It does look like a spring with a pool beneath. And there, just above it, is a shelf with an overhang that could lead to a cave. It looks small, but I think we could manage to maneuver into it. At least that would provide shelter for our landing craft and it's closer to the surface than we are now."

"Yes, I see that. It looks to be closer to the continental shores of this area as well. I just hope we aren't about to invade the lair of a ferocious beast. I'm not up to slaying dragons right now."

"Nor am I," Troy agreed with a chuckle. "I don't think there are dragons in existence on earth anymore. Did you see the size of those fish that came close as we were outside? They seem be total accepting of us. I think they may have been a dolphin species but certainly larger than the ones I remember seeing on Fentanys. We were told the flora and fauna would not be troubled by us and it seems they are fine with our being here, so relax, okay?"

"Let's try to settle our craft there then. Can you do that?" Brad asked.

"Yes, it's small, but with a slow, careful maneuver we should be able to do it." Troy agreed as he watched the dials and camera angles then pressed a button and pushed levers to slowly moved the craft off the shelf on which it sat. It dropped suddenly, but with a daft thrust, Troy made it rise slowly upward and to the left toward the shelf they had seen above the springs.

"I'll make one pass. Check the depth of the indent. If it looks wide enough, we will settle in there."

"It looks likes a long shallow indent in the rock wall below the overhang, not a cave at all, but I think it will be workable if you edge her in sideways. Go ahead and land there if you can, Troy."

Troy lowered the craft again, then made it rise slowly and veer toward the wall at an angle. Fish and other species scattered away from the rock wall as the craft lifted and edged closer. The Landing Craft from Xernex appears to be circular in shape when in flight, partly due to its rotative motion, but when stationary it resembles a squat, plump cylinder with a slightly flattened top. Troy fully concentrated as he worked the levers and dials to move the craft closer and extend the landing gear.

"You may want to rotate so the exit hatch extends toward the outer lip of the ledge," Cee suggested.

"Right," Troy agreed. The craft dropped again as he made that correction. Troy brought it up again and in position parallel to the opening then slowly, carefully edged it under the overhang. "The ceiling of the overhang is rough and lower than I thought," he complained as he lowered the landing gear to half mast and pushed the thrust lever ever so carefully. The water caused some resistance at first, but then rushed around and out as the mass of the craft displaced the water in the alcove. Troy swiped beads of sweat from his forehead, raised the landing gear and let the craft settle gently on the smooth surface of the ledge.

"Wow! That was impressive, Troy," Brad extolled with a wide grin.

"Excellent maneuver, sir," Cee agreed.

Troy exhaled deeply and leaned back with a grin. "Thanks guys. Ah, Brad can you calculate our exact coordinates? I will need to report them to Central Control. And we will need to see what is to be done with E…with the body. We have no means of cremating so I'm not sure what protocol is required here."

"No, no one told us what to do in case of a casualty in these circumstances, did they?" Brad agreed sadly.

Reception was poor, so they had to move a communications receptor filament out from under the ledge before they could communicate properly. Peter wasn't in a better a mood when Troy eventually reported they were settled and gave the coordinates. When asked about the protocol for dealing with the body, Peter was stymied and called to his supervisor for aid.

"Has her family been notified? Do they have any specific wishes?" Brad asked.

"Sit tight. We will get back to you on that," was the answer they got.

"Humans here on earth have performed sea burials," Cee commented. "It requires that the body be weighted down; it may rise after a time as gasses form upon decomposition. However, there is historical evidence of such burials. The salinity of the water and prevailing currents need to be considered when dumping a body into the sea."

"Thank you, Cee," Troy said. Then he turned to Brad. "I did notice that the water here is more buoyant than that on Fentanys and the ocean currents are stronger."

"Yes, these oceans would be more saline. I'm very anxious to do some exploring once all this is settled. We don't have to surface and start melding with the human population immediately, do we? I'd like to do some research here where we are first," Brad said.

His background specialty was micro-biology, so he was obviously curious about how the reported pollution effected flora and fauna in the water. "Our mission is to evaluate the pollutions problems on earth, so why not start with the ocean environment?" Brad continued.

Troy replied, "I agree; we can get to the human population later to ascertain what, if anything, they are doing to alleviate the problem. But for now, I suggest we fuel up with some food and water then get some rest. How is the arm feeling, Brad?"

"Sore but bearable; how's your head?"

"Tender but okay," Troy replied.

"Hard," Cee said in his best English butler voice at the same time. Then he said staidly, "I shall return with your repast shortly," before turning and exiting the room.

Brad roared with laughter. "However, did you program him to do that?"

Troy chuckled as well. "I don't remember exactly how it all started, but Cee gets a kick out of doing that old English butler schtick. If a robot can get a kick out of anything, that is. But it is a great tension reducer, you must admit."

"Oh, I do agree," Brad replied still chuckling.

"I wonder what Peter's problem is; he certainly is surly on communication. Peter is often, well, taciturn, I guess you would say, but why so surly today?" Troy mused aloud.

"Maybe he is still miffed about not having been chosen to work on one of the landing crews. I heard he was hoping to be included but I think the directors made a good choice in having him in communications. That's his forte after all. Or it has to do with the mess that will result from Ling's behavior. I gather he and Ling were quite friendly."

"Oh, I didn't know that," Troy said.

Brad laughed, "Troy, you are always too busy to sit around and chat. I'm not surprised you aren't up on the latest gossip on Xernex."

Troy leaned forward and said eagerly, "I've got time now, so clue me in on the latest!"

The men chatted amiably as they ate the meal Cee had brought, which included additional vitamins and minerals that would help their bodies to heal. Before retiring, they performed their usual meditations, calling on the Universal Life Force energy to assist with their healing as well. Then Brad excused himself, "I'm for bed. Do we take the submersible out tomorrow and look around a bit?"

Troy thought a bit then decided, "No, let's do a recon of the local area manually first before venturing further afield with the sub."

Laying on his sleeping pellet later that evening, Troy realized he should have been paying more attention to the personal lives of the crew. His uncle had asked that he watch things. After chatting with Brad, he recognized that though he was always friendly with the crew and was well received by them, he may have missed some important clues by not paying closer attention to the personal tidbits and gossip. A good lesson to remember when dealing with the human population as well, he knew.

Chapter 5

Kevin sat in the departure lounge of the Powell River Airport awaiting the early morning shuttle back to Vancouver. His father, Wayne Warden, had picked him up earlier, after John had ferried him from Savary Island to the marina here, and driven him to the airport. Rachael and the children would be traveling back to Vancouver in a week.

Kevin relaxed in his chair and tried to get his mind back in work-mode after the holiday. Rachael had asked him to stop by the therapy pool where she and another pediatric nurse supervised a program wherein disabled and mentally dysfunctional children got to swim and play with dolphins and other sea mammals on loan from the aquarium. He needed to check into the research project he was involved with at the Vancouver Aquarium anyway, so he'd stop by there before heading out to his office at the University of British Columbia, Kevin decided.

A group of noisy young people entering the departure area caught his attention. Several were carrying cases that looked to be musical instruments - a guitar and violin or fiddle, and possibly a banjo, Kevin thought. He smiled to himself, remembering the days when he and his band, River Rock, had travel like that. One of the girls in the group took the chair beside him, dropping her bags and instrument case at her feet with a sigh.

"Was your band up here for a gig or are you heading to Vancouver for one?" Kevin asked in his usual gravelly voice. She turned to him with a puzzled frown.

"No, we are part of the Texada High School band going to a competition in Chilliwack. Our band won the local competition. Now we are off to the provincial finals," she stated proudly.

"That is impressive. Good luck at the competitions," Kevin replied warmly as the stewardess announced boarding.

Kevin buckled into the window seat watching the ocean below as the plane banked over the Malaspina Strait and headed south. The ocean was clear and calm - a perfect summer day, just as they had all been for most of the family vacation, he reflected. Ancion's visit on Friday had been a great bonus. He chuckled quietly thinking on how, as John had predicted, Rachael was annoyed at having missed that. A question asked by the young girl who he had spoken with earlier caught his attention as she leaned past the young man in the center seat beside him.

"Did you ever live on Texada Island, sir?" she asked tentatively.

"Yes, I did live there until in my early teens when my family moved over to Powell River. Why do you ask?" Kevin said kindly.

She blushed a bit, glancing at the fellow in the center seat. "I told you," she said to him then turned back to Kevin. "You are Kevin Warden, aren't you? The dolphin rescuer, right? And you played trumpet in a band with the Ortega twins, didn't you?" she stammered, blushing again.

"Yes, I am Kevin Warden, and the Ortega twins and I did form a band, River Rock, after I moved to Powell River. We played at the Texada Island High School prom years ago when Effie, Miss Simmons, was the music teacher there."

"Wow! It's awesome to meet you, sir," the fellow in the center said, sticking out his hand.

Kevin laughed and shook his hand and that of the girl at the end of the row. "And you are?" he asked the girl.

"Jenny Stinger. My dad works at the mine, but he wasn't from here. Mom told us about your band and what a hero you were…are…" she gushed.

"Jimmy Abbott," the young man said by way of introduction, "and you and a professor at UBC are now advocates for cleaning up the oceans. Our teachers told us about that."

Humbled at such adoration, Kevin paused for a moment, not sure how to reply to these eager youngsters. "The talks Professor Fitzhugh and I attended were a success, yes. An International Coalition assisted by a Dutch Company, utilizing technology created right here at UBC, has develop a technique that hopefully will help rid the oceans of those huge pools of garbage. I am sure you have heard about it. But," he added, "a project like that takes a lot of dedication and demanding work by many talented people working together. I'm no hero, just one of the team."

Jenny and Jimmy kept peppering him with questions about his work, about working with dolphins, and about how he and the Ortega's got their own band started, until the stewardess announced arrival in Vancouver.

Jenny foraged in her bag until she found a notebook. "May I have your autograph, Mr. Warden?" she asked. "It has been great talking with you and I'm sure my mom will be thrilled to hear we met you. My mom was Sharon Bickman before she married dad."

Kevin wasn't sure what to write, then settled on 'Nice to meet you, Jenny. Good luck in the Band Competitions' and signed his full name. Then he turned to Jimmy, shook his hand, and wished him well.

"Sharon Bickman," Kevin mused as he sat in the cab rushing towards the city and his home in North Vancouver. He had not heard anything about her after the incident at prom where she got in trouble with police because of drugs and alcohol. She must have straightened up her life after that if her daughter was any indication. Jenny seemed like an intelligent, honest, and courteous young lady. That was good to know, and he would remember to share this tidbit with the Ortega twins when he saw them again. But, right now he would unload his holiday gear, grab a bite to eat and drive over to the aquarium, then to his office at UBC to clue Fritz in on the latest and catch up on his projects. Back to work!

Chapter 6

Troy was surprised that after he'd reported to command the next morning, it was Syvers, one of his instructors, who answered.

"Thank you, Troy. You appear to be settled there now. Good."

"What of the others, sir?" Troy asked.

The instructor hesitated then answered tersely, "Both Raj and Maria have made a safe landing. Raj has found himself to be in the middle of a war zone. Some local conflict, he thinks. Maria is happily monitoring the flora and fauna of an African desert and hasn't contacted humans yet. Ling will not be evacuating to earth. She and Peter, who appears to have been one of her cohorts, are under guard."

"I see," Troy replied. "Will another crew be deployed to the South China sea?"

"That is still being debated pending further investigation," Syvers said, "and as to the disposal of…uh…the corpse, a sea burial would be appropriate. Her family would appreciate you bring along her personal items to Xernex when you return."

"Yes, of course. We can do that," Troy replied solemnly.

"Good. We will not be sending a replacement, so you and Brad will need to carry on. Have you formulated a plan of action?"

"Yes sir," Troy replied with more enthusiasm, "firstly, we have found the flora and fauna of the oceans here are not averse to our presence, and the oceans here have greater salinity than those on Fentanys. Brad and I have decided to explore the oceanic milieu before venturing up to integrate amongst the humans. We will be reporting our findings."

"Excellent plan; proceed."

"So that's why Peter was so terse yesterday," Brad commented when Troy related what Syvers had told him. "I wonder what they had planned and to whom they are reporting. Do we, too, need to be watchful of other hostile off-planetary beings while here on Earth? I certainly didn't sign up for having to deal with other than Earth beings while here. They may be challenging enough without having to deal with hostile alien beings as well. We have come in peace and merely as observers, after all."

"You have a point there, Brad," Troy observed. "I wish I could have a chat with the commander about this. But let's not worry unduly about that until we learn more. Also, I would like to contact Maria and Raj directly, but from what was said and the way he said it, I deduce that there is still a ban on communication. I'll ask about that next time I report in."

"Yes, do that." Brad sighed, "Now, I guess our first task is to consign Ellen's body to a resting place, right?"

"Agreed," Troy said sadly, "We will have to do some sort of make-shift sea burial. Cee can help us with that, I think. You do know that her spirit lives and will find it's true home no matter where in the universes her physical body perishes, don't you Brad?"

Brad nodded and said, "Yes, that's what are taught. But you know Troy, I've never had to face death so directly before. You were still unconscious when we eventually settled after the crash. If Cee hadn't assured me her vitals showed she was dead, I'd have not known how to handle it. It was much easier for me to do the assessment of damage to the ship than deal with her body." Brad slumped in his chair, fidgeted with his hands and looked at his feet.

Troy leaned over, placing his hand on Brad's arm. "Hey, my friend, you handled it all well. No one can fault your actions. Facing the death of a mission mate isn't an easy thing, is it? We have both known her and worked with her for years. Elyngtren was one of the family, and we will miss her."

Brad glanced up and said softly, "Thank you for that Troy. We will miss her - her enthusiasm for the mission and her excitement at being here. It is so sad she isn't going to experience this. And, did you know that she planned for this to be her last off-planet mission? She said that she has a significant other on Fentanys, and they planned to form a family unit and produce offspring after she returned. Ellen has been part of other interplanetary missions, but this earth landing was to be her dream fulfilled. So sad!"

"Yes," Troy replied softly, "we can honor her by completing this mission to the best of our ability as she would have done. Now, let's get Cee to help us with the burial."

"And thank the One God for Cee!" Brad replied with a soft chuckle.

"Do we have DPIs on board, sir?" Cee asked.

"Yes, that could work," Troy reflected. Diplopyroisoliate is a clear, heavy and highly inflammable metallic substance, an amalgam of pyrolusite, which is found in boggy areas and in hydrothermal deposits. It was the practice on Fentanys to place the dead in opaque bags made of DPI at a funeraria after the life force energy had left the body. These body bags were then placed on display for a time, so friends and families could say farewell to the departed before they were slid into huge ovens for cremation.

"Yes, I think we do have sheets of DPIs aboard that are used to help in the repair of the outer Plasmodial Shield," Brad replied thoughtfully, obviously following Troy's train of thought. "Perhaps we could make a sort of 'body bag' of one of these, but we need something to weigh the body down."

"A cleat or two inside the bag with El…with the body should do it," Troy replied, "They are heavy enough." These "cleats" are heavy magnetic, metallic shoes that are attached to the landing gear to keep the craft stable.

"Sounds like a plan. Let's get it done," Brad said with a sigh.

It didn't take long to accomplish the task, insert the body, and maneuver the body bag close to the outer hatch. Before donning their aquatic gear, Troy asked, "Brad, do you remember the words for the Consignment Ceremony?"

"The words to … what?"

"You know…the ceremony whereby the life force energy of the departed is consigned back to the Creator God."

Brad hung his head and said, "Troy, I haven't been to a funeral since I was a small child, so no, I don't remember the words.

"Cee?" Troy asked.

"I'll research it, sir."

After the men had donned their aquatic gear, Cee came forward and repeated the beautiful words of the Consignment Ceremony in his English butler accent. That made the men smile even as they pushed the bag out the hatch and over the ledge. Both stood in silence as the body sank. The large sea mammals they had noticed earlier hovered close by. Several seem to be following the funeral bag downward. One swam close enough to nudge Troy gently, clicking and whistling urgently. Troy glanced at the large beast, then nervously motioned to Brad. They quickly returned to their craft.

"Cee did a superb job of researching and reciting the words of the Consignment Ceremony, didn't he?" Brad commented.

"Yes, he did," Troy ruminated. "You know, the humans here on earth are well advanced in technology and knowledge. They must have some sort of system like our central data banks. Once we can decipher the frequency of their communications systems, I'll program Cee to monitor things through them directly, rather than having to go through the Earth specialists on Fentanys."

"Good plan!" Brad cheered, "We could even get Cee to peruse the local news media to catch up on the latest. Ellen would have loved to be part of this type of thing. Communications, as well as Navigations, were her areas of expertise after all."

The men spent a somber evening remembering Ellen, sorting through her personal effects for what they thought her family may want. "We can store these in her locker until we return to Xernex," Troy said. "Now, let us get some rest. I told Syvers we planned to do some exploring in the area before attempting to meet with the human population."

"That suits me," Brad replied. "Did you notice how large some of those fish...dolphin I think...are? And how badly some of their skin was marked and scarred?"

"No, I hadn't noticed. But they seem interested in us. The big one seems to want to 'chat', but I find I feel rather intimidated by their bulk," Troy admitted sheepishly.

"You? Troy, our intrepid leader, afraid of a mere dolphin?" Brad teased. "Didn't you tell us of a trip you and your family took to the ocean when you were younger? You said your parents let you play with them, and your father taught you to communicate with the sea-life?"

"True, but these guys are much bigger and may not understand our 'language'."

"Troy!" Brad exclaimed," Just think. If you could make contact, it would be a tremendous aid to our mission."

"How so?"

"We could research the dolphins here on Earth. If they wander the oceans as the Fentanys sea-life do, they could show us some of the areas of greatest damage in the waters. This we then report back," Brad raised his brow, "simple."

Troy laughed and raised his hands in a ceding gesture. "Ok, we go out exploring these local waters tomorrow and I'll see if I can "chat" with the big guy."

The next day both men suited up in their aquatic gear and ventured out to explore the area around their landing craft. They hadn't encountered any of the large dolphins, but Brad was particularly excited about their findings and reported to Mothership Xernex immediately upon returning to their craft.

"These oceans have greater salinity and are more buoyant than I'd thought, and the currents are quite strong. I think we should use a tethering line between us next time we venture out," Troy commented.

"Yes, I agree, but I wish I had a better lab facility on board," Brad groused. Today's findings are remarkable! I'd love to study Earth's aquatic flora and fauna in greater detail."

"Perhaps once we contact the human population, you can find such a facility. I didn't notice a lot of pollution around this area, did you? Though some of the rock formations were littered with a whitish over-coating that seemed odd, and one area had an oily slime adhering to it. Did you notice that?" Troy asked.

"Yes, and I reported on it and the coordinates involved. Should we take out the submersible craft or do more manual observations tomorrow?"

"Manual for now," Troy decided.

The next day, after attaching a tethering line, Troy and Brad ventured out again, moving closer to the landmass and upward. At first, engrossed in their observations they did not notice the dolphins who hovered nearby. "Troy, why don't you try to 'chat' with the big guy while I recon that rise above us," Brad commented when he became aware of their presence.

Troy slowly moved closer to the animal, trying to figure out how to approach the dolphin. The animal angled close, gently nudging Troy, squeaking and whistling urgently.

"Would you like to speak with me?" Troy asked telepathically. The animal swam away nervously, then approached again. Troy tried it again, mentally rephrasing to a loose translation of Common but still in the English of the area. "Speak with us, you would?"

"Click, click."

"An affirmative that is?"

"Click, click."

Excited now, Troy tried again, mentally asking if their presence was a danger to the animal.

"Click."

"A negative that is."

"Click, Click"

Wow, this is amazing, Troy thought excitedly as he moved even closer to one side, near the eye, of the beast. Looking directly into that eye he felt...what?...a kinship, a brotherhood. Troy reached up above the eye to stroke the dolphin's soft skin. The huge beast seemed to smile, then with a click and a chirp he rose high in the water, plunged again, then moved to join the others.

Dazed and a bit shaken, Troy floated toward where Brad was collecting water samples in his testing kit. Sensing Troy's preoccupied mind, Brad led the way back to their craft in silence. Once there and settled with refreshments, Troy told Brad about his communication with the big male dolphin.

The next morning, they found the dolphins circling restlessly around the alcove where their craft sat. "They are certainly out in full force. I wonder what's happening," Brad commented.

Troy shrugged and said, "I'll suit up and step out and see if I can find out. I'd like to take the submersible and go further afield today if you agree with that, Brad. We could spot land nearby or at least find a cavern closer to the continental shore. We will need to contact humans soon."

Brad looked distressed. He said, "There is still much to study here. I'd like to work in this area a little longer."

Again, Troy shrugged noncommittedly and said, "But meanwhile, I'll try to find out what's going on outside."

Two things registered with Troy immediately: First, the ocean was much more turbulent than before. Currents were stronger and the water was more turbid. Secondly, the big guy was clicking and whistling loudly, and he came right up to Troy as he stepped out onto the ledge.

"Amiss something is?" he said telepathically.

"Click...Click."

Puzzled by the response, Troy tried again.

"Help we can?"

"Click, click."

"For you there is danger?"

The dolphin rose high and seemed to glance back, hoping Troy would follow. What is it? Troy glanced around and observed more carefully. The waters were very turbid and currents strong. Had something occurred above them, a storm, a tidal wave? He wished that he could figure out how to speak with the big guy more clearly.

"In these waters, danger there is?"

"Come you must! A cutting stick you have... knife?"

Good, we are communicating. Wow! "Click, click," Troy answered.

"Bring, come," The dolphin swam slowly upward.

"Wait! Follow in our other craft we will, lead us you would."

"Click, click."

"Brad, come back to the craft immediately," Troy urged, speaking into his communicator.

"What is it?" Brad replied.

"I'm not sure, but I think the dolphins need us; he asked me to bring a knife."

Brad's eyes widened in alarm, "Are you sure about this, Troy?"

"Yes, I sense a definite urgency. We will take the submersible and follow the dolphin to whatever it is that is troubling them. Cee, stay on board, and I will keep you informed of our situation."

As soon as Brad returned with his samples, the men quickly prepared and launched the submersible. Troy edged it toward the waiting dolphin. He stared at the big guy. "Lead us you will?"

"Click, click."

The pod moved quickly upward and to the left, keeping the sub surrounded with their bulky bodies. After a time, the waters seemed shallower. Brad reported their coordinates back to Cee as Troy carefully maneuvered around large rocks on the shoreline. The dolphins parted, and he saw the problem just ahead. A huge beast, like a dolphin but much larger, seemed to be in great distress, heaving about, churning up the water outside a small inlet. Other giants like it milled about nearby.

"You stay inside for now, Brad. I'll anchor the sub just below the surface then try to find out what the problem is."

"Okay," Brad replied a little dubiously, as he surveyed the scene.

Troy chuckled, "Hey, we made contact and found land. Let me be the 'intrepid commander' and do what needs to be done."

The moment he stepped out of the sub, the big guy was there, urging him forward. The other animals, even the ones of the other species, seemed to give way, allowing the dolphin and Troy to pass. "Help! Untangle whale. Breathe she must!"

Ah, now Troy realized what was needed. The large animal was enmeshed in some sort of netted material unable to free itself. Therefore...the knife. "Click, click. Free her I shall. Lay quietly she must," Troy said to the dolphin.

"Brad, we have a stranded animal, a whale. Get Cee to find out what he can about this species, then come join me. Bring your diamond-edged knife."

"Be right there. Ah, can you send your buddy to escort me through the throng?"

"Will do," Troy said with a chuckle even as he edged closer to the whale. Oh, she truly was entangled. Moving toward animal's head, Troy stood chest deep in the water near the animal's eye. He felt for the meshing, speaking telepathically in soft, soothing tones. The whale calmed down some, stopped thrashing about, and the other animals moved back to give him space to work. Troy wasn't familiar with the meshing material, but the diamond-edged knife sliced through it quite easily. Brad joined him and began cutting away the offending material from the others side of the animal's head. She grunted and quivered some but remained still.

When they had freed some of the material, they tried to roll it back and off the animal. When they had rolled the mesh free of her blowhole, the whale heaved a huge sigh and blew a large smelly spume into the air. She wriggled to try, it seemed, to help remove the offending material and to maneuver herself off the sand and into the deeper waters. Both men had to move quickly out of her way.

"Wow, this whale is huge. Tell it to calm down, Troy. It nearly crushed me!" Brad cried.

Troy again moved toward the one eye, telepathically sending soothing light energy to the animal. She sighed, blew spume, and became still again. The men worked steadily and as quickly as they could, cutting away the mesh and rolling it off the poor beast's body. The whale seemed to understand what was needed and she moved gently to assist when she could.

"Troy, it seems we have human company," Brad informed him.

"I noticed; the dolphins and whales are staying clear of the shore near the human. We'll watch it carefully. I think we almost have this lady cleared. If the humans aren't hostile, I'd like to have a look on shore."

Brad responded, "She is badly scarred but mobile, I think. I wish we could examine her more fully. Whales are akin to dolphins according to Cee. They often swim together though some species prey upon dolphins."

"Very interesting!" exclaimed Troy.

The men moved away, allowing the huge animal space to wriggle itself into deeper water. Some of the dolphins followed. However, the big guy and a few others stayed close by as the men bundled up the dangerous mesh.

"Who are you? What do you think you are doing in my bay?" yelled the human male angrily, as he strode toward them. "You are trespassing. I suggest you leave now!"

Troy shoved his headgear and facemask up and over his head to dangle down his back as he turned to the man and slowly walked closer. Brad followed. When they were only a few feet away, Troy said calmly, "You observed what we did - we freed a strangled whale in this bay. Now, if you will just help us dispose of this offending mesh material, we will leave your bay."

"Just chuck it back in the ocean and go."

"No!" Brad exclaimed angrily, "And have another poor misfortunate animal damaged by it? There must be another way to destroy it safely."

"Christ! Another bunch of bleeding-hearts, nature loving do-gooders," the man threw up his arms in disgust and turned to stomp away. "Just you get yourselves out of my bay," he yelled over his shoulder, then he stopped and turned back to peer at Troy more closely. Troy stood quietly at alert, refusing to be intimidated.

Another younger male human came bounding down the sand toward them. "What's up, dad?" the younger one shouted as he neared. The older man waved his son away as he walked closer to Troy.

"You! You're one of those bloody dolphin-whisperers!" he accused, poking Troy none-to-gently on the chest with an extended finger. "Christ, you even look like Kevin Warden. You a relative or something?"

"Wow, dad this is great! Nice to meet you mister," he said enthusiastically, "I saw you chatting with the whale. And Dad look, that dolphin with the notched dorsal fin is hovering nearby."

Troy and Brad began to relax. They had made human contact and with ones who knew or were familiar with Troy's holographic clone. What luck!!

"Mister?" Brad asked, "If you would just show us how to destroy this netting we will be away, out of your bay.

"Oh sure, it's too torn up to be of use, right Dad? I'll burn it in the incinerator," the younger man agreed. "But are you a relative of Kevin's?" he asked Troy. Troy debated about how much to reveal…what to say?

"Troy is a distant relative of a Kevin Warden," Brad answered for him, "but they have never met. This is our first time on...in this area."

The big dolphin whistled sharply from the bay and Troy turned toward the water.

"Thank you for your assistance," he said to the boy, handing him the bundle of netting. He turned to the elder, "We will be on our way."

"Just you stay our of my bay," he grumbled, "Bloody bleeding hearts!"

"But dad...this is really exciting, what if..."

"Just you shut your mouth. No chatting about this here incident either, right Junior? Don't want strangers messing about here, now do we?"

"Yes pa… I mean, no we don't."

Troy and Brad stood silently in the bay watching as the two men walked back into the surrounding forest. “Let’s walk the shore to where the sub is anchored,” Troy said. “I’d like to examine this area a bit more thoroughly before we leave.”

“Okay,” Brad agreed. Troy turned back to speak with the dolphin briefly. The big guy thanked him for his assistance, then with a powerful leap high into the air and a loud whistle, he plunged and rushed to join the others.

Chapter 7

Both Troy and Brad sat in reflective silence as Troy guided the sub back to their landing craft using the coordinates Brad had recorded when they had followed the dolphins. Freeing the poor whale, who had been entangled in some sort of mesh, hadn't been difficult given the assistance from the dolphins and the efficiency of their own diamond edged knives, called quistyrs.

These knives are unique to Fentanys as far as Troy knew. Quistyrs are short double-edged narrow blades made of a strong metal or metallic alloy. Coarse diamond dust is annealed into one of the sides of the blade to give it strength and a serrated edge. The hilt of the quistyr bares the unique symbol of the owner's ancestry, and it is given to a young teenager as a merit of honor within the family unit when he or she attains adulthood. As he had many times before, Troy felt deep gratitude to have been honored thusly, and he was glad to have had this instrument in his possession today.

The meeting with the humans did seem fortunate but troubling as well. Troy realized they would need to analyze this event more closely and decide how to use it, what they could learn from it. Each landing unit had its own back-story, a well-formulated history with documentation to prove it. And each team member had their own personal one as well. Now they needed to integrate these with what they had learned today. More observation would be needed, Troy decided.

"The father and son seemed to recognize your dolphin friend," Brad commented, interrupting Troy's musings.

"Yes, they did. Maybe the dolphin can shed some light on that. I will need to go through Kevin's history in greater detail. I remember that, like me, as a boy he also befriended dolphins. Our Earth experts may know something about that as well. Perhaps that's the place to start."

"While you are at it, perhaps find out what that mesh material is, what it is used for, and how it got to be in the ocean. My guess is pollution - waste dumping. If that is the case, it's so awful, so careless and thoughtless. And those two humans weren't even concerned about it! The whale must have been beached some time earlier, and no one helped her. No wonder Earth sent a cry for help!"

"Yes, it is awful, Brad, but I have a feeling we will be seeing more of this kind of thing. We will need to corollate our findings, and I will report to Syvers first thing in the morning."

***

The next morning, after they had reported to Syvers and were commended on aiding the whale and contacting the Earth humans, Ben, the Commander of Xernex, their mothership, and Troy's uncle, contacted them. "Troy, Brad, let me congratulate you both on your fine work there," he commented. "And Troy, do you think you can speak with that dolphin again? Brad is correct in that the denizens of the oceans could assist you in evaluating the degree of pollution in the oceans of Earth. The other two landing parties have done well in assessing the land and air pollution. As well, if this dolphin does know of Kevin Warden and where he may live, it could help you find a way meet him and perhaps ease your way into the human population that way."

"Yes, I had thought of that, but I cannot just call the dolphin, you know. He comes and goes as he chooses," Troy replied.

Ben chuckled and said, "So, you can't control everything, young man. Be patient. Meanwhile, find a spot close to shore to moor your landing craft, and the two of you go ahead and discover the ocean."

"That will work. Brad wanted to do more research underwater anyway, before we ventured onto land. Have you heard anything more from...of my father?" Troy asked tentatively.

"No, son. I had hoped you had made further contact," Ben replied carefully.

"I will try," Troy agreed.

"Good," Ben replied. "Carry on then you two. Good work. Stay safe."

Brad cheered, "Yes! Let's find a safe place to anchor closer to land and get to work studying the water here."

Chapter 8

At his summons, Kevin stepped into Professor Dennis Fitzhugh's office right on time. Fritz, as he was known to all his close associates, was on the phone and signalled for Kevin to have a seat. Kevin took a moment to study his mentor. The man had looked old to him when they had met almost twenty years earlier, and he looked even older now but was working as hard as ever. Kevin, in his concern for the man, had taken on more and more of the workload, but it seemed neither of them had enough hours in the day to accomplish what needed to be done. Kevin sighed and glanced at the clock behind Fritz's desk.

"Stop fidgeting, Kevin," Fritz growled, "the Chinese delegate cancelled the meeting for today and tabled for next week. I gave him your report. He will peruse it and give us his yay or nay then. You did well with that research and documented all thoroughly, so just relax now."

"I know, but we really need China on board if we are going to get an opportunity to try the new Dutch invention for oceanic pollution removal in the South China Sea."

"Oh, they will come on board," Fritz chuckled. "It would be to their detriment politically not to do so. So, what are you and the family planning to do for this coming long weekend?"

Kevin smiled and said, "The wife and kids have commitments here in Vancouver, but John and I thought to take the yacht out and do some fishing, then close the cabin on Savary Island for the winter. We thought to leave early Friday morning and return Monday afternoon. The weather is predicted to be favorable over the weekend." He glanced at Fritz speculatively. "Fancy a bit of fishing out in the Georgia Strait?"

Fritz steepled his hands under his chin and regarded Kevin thoughtfully. "You know, I've not been out on the water in some time. I'd enjoy a bit of fishing, thank you."

Later that evening, after Kevin got home and spoke to his wife, Rachael, she crowed, "Wow, you got the old goat to leave his desk for a few days!"

"Honey, he's not an old goat," Kevin admonished his wife playfully, "but it would do him a world of good to relax a bit, soak in some sun."

"Would be good for you too," she said on a sigh, "You work too hard too, dear. I wish I could go along. Last time you and dad went out fishing you met up with the dolphins and had all the fun without me."

"You could get your assistants to cover for you and join us," he suggested.

"No, I've worked too hard to hand the project over to someone else now. And I need to finish sewing up Keira's costume for the dress rehearsal for her school play on Monday, remember? And Greg has a soccer game on Monday as well. No, you men run along and enjoy!"

***

The sun streaked the sky in pinky hues over the coastal mountains behind Vancouver as John steered the yacht out of the harbor and headed northwest. The air was crisp and cool, the ocean calm and glassy in the morning light. Kevin sat on deck savoring a cup of coffee.

"Ah, now this is the life!" he exclaimed, and he breathed in the cool salty air.

Fritz chuckled and agreed, "It is! Thank you for inviting me along."

"You're welcome," John replied from at the helm, "but we expect you to pull your own weight here on board, old man, and lure in some big fish," he added with a teasing chuckle.

Fritz grunted, leaned back on the chair, crossed his arms over his massive chest, pulled his hat down over his brow and proceeded to snooze.

Kevin was at the helm later as they sailed past Hernando Island toward Savary. Boat traffic was light in the area, and they were making good time. The men had agreed to push on to the cabin today and set out fishing early the next day. John and Fritz sat on the deck relaxing and chatting easily.

"Kevin," John called, "grab your binoculars. There seems to be a pod of dolphins off the south coast of Hernando Island."

"I see them," Kevin cried excitedly. "You guys want to sail closer and take a look?"

Kevin steered the boat toward the area.

Fritz was peering through his binoculars as well. "Good heavens, there are a lot of them, and they are very close to the shore. They seem agitated about something."

"This side of Hernando is quite uninhabited, but I think I see some sort of water-craft beached there."

A few of the dolphins broke away from the melee and swam directly toward the yacht.

"John," Kevin called, "come take the helm. I think that may be Ancion."

A large dolphin rose high in the air beside the yacht, clicking and whistling loudly.

"Look - the notched fin!" Fritz cried. "Talk to him, Kevin."

Kevin stood at the side of the boat and watched as Ancion approached. "Ancion?"

"Click, click."

"Yeah, it's him," he cried. "Hello buddy." He reached out to touch the big animal who swam beside them.

"Quiven, help, must."

Kevin clicked questioningly.

"Human, injured. Come you must."

"Click, click. Follow we will."

"John," he called, "there seems to be a boater in danger up ahead. Anchor as close to that cove as you can. I'll suit up and follow the dolphins."

"Aye, will do," John replied.

"I'll don my diving gear and join you. Damn, if you and that dolphin don't always find trouble, young man," Fritz growled.

Kevin and Fritz followed Ancion to the cove. A young man stood beside an odd-looking craft, waving at them. He pushed the headgear of his equally odd-looking diving suit off his head as they approached.

"Thank you for stopping," he said in a weak voice. "My shipmate is injured and in need of medical assistance. Can you help us?"

"Certainly," Fritz replied briskly. "Is he mobile?"

"No, Brad has a badly infected gash on his leg. He is delirious with fever. Nothing I do seems to help."

Kevin glanced around, "Is your eh, boat, operational? Can you bring him to the yacht?" he asked, pointing toward where John had anchored.

"Yes," Troy replied weakly, as he swayed dangerously.

Kevin rushed forward to grab him, "Here let me help you." Together they moved toward craft. It appeared to be a sort of 2-man mini-submarine.

The three men sized up the situation quickly. This young man was also injured but alert. The other lay silently in a captain's chair.

"Kevin, you join this young fellow in the sub. I'll head back to the yacht. Maybe we can use the grappling hook to haul this baby aboard, then get them both to hospital in Powell River."

"Good plan, Fritz," Kevin turned to the young man. "What are your injuries? Can you drive this craft to the yacht?"

"Yes, I can," Troy replied in a soft hiss. "Head injury - stopped bleeding - bad headache - possible concussion. I am Troy Gillis."

He extended his hand toward Kevin who shook it firmly and said, "Kevin Warden."

They managed to get the sub onboard the yacht and get both Troy and Brad out of their diving gear. “Thank you,” Troy said softly then collapsed into unconsciousness.

John alerted the Powell River Marina of the situation and had arranged for two ambulances to stand by. Fritz rifled through the men’s clothing to find small pouches on each of them that contained only a few Canadian dollars and passports - nothing more. Fritz and Kevin sat with the men in the forward cabin as John sped the yacht toward Powell River.

“Curious situation here, don’t you think Kevin?” Fritz remarked. “Brad and Troy have little I.D. on them. Their sub and equipment are state-of-the art, even perhaps a prototype or experimental watercraft, I think.”

“Yes, and their last stop was somewhere in South Africa, according to their passports. How did they land up here on Canadian shores?”

“Blaze…move it, Troy. Get us out of here! Hot!” Brad mumbled then quieted again.

“Almost to PR. How are the guys doing?” John shouted down to them. Troy grabbed Kevin’s arm and tried to sit up.

“Easy man,” Kevin said quietly as he gently tried to push Troy back onto the bed.

Troy resisted. “Hide submersible and our gear,” he whispered urgently. “Could be in danger. Hide sub! Call Central Command!” he cried and tried to push Kevin away. Once again, he tried to get up, then fell back into a coma.

“Fritz, put their stuff in the sub and pull a tarp over it, before we get to the harbor.”

"Kevin, do you think that's wise? The authorities..."

"Do it, Fritz," Kevin hissed.

Fritz studied Kevin for a moment then went topside to do as he was asked.

Once they had docked, the two men were whisked away to the hospital in a flurry of activity. Kevin gave the paramedics the little information they had.

"Luckily you folks found these fellows when you did," one of the paramedics commented, "strong winds and high-water warnings for tonight."

The men agreed that John and Fritz would push on to Savary Island, stow the boat in the boathouse and batten down the hatches before the storm. Kevin had called his father to pick him up. He would check on the men in hospital and stay in Powell River for the night in case he was needed.

Chapter 9

Troy slowly became aware of sounds around him and pain... extreme pain in his head. He tried to open his eyes, but the light seared through him in waves of agony, so he closed them again and tried to lift his hand up to his head to feel what was happening.

"No, don't touch," a female voice urged softly, "Eventually joining us, are you? Are you in pain?"

Troy lowered his hand with an audible groan. So weak...he was so very weak; he could barely move.

A hand touched his shoulder gently, and the same female voice said, "Just relax young man. Can you hear me? Don't open your eyes yet. I'll get you some medicine for the pain. A doctor will be with you shortly."

A few minutes later, the pain eased some, and Troy drifted off again into a dark, empty world. Darkness, lacking any sensation, engulfed him; then a distant sound seemed to penetrate. Troy concentrated on that sound until he recognized a voice - the voice of his father.

"Dad?" Troy tried to speak the word, but he couldn't; he wasn't alert enough yet to do so.

"Yes, it is I, son," came the voice again, distinct and gentle like a breeze floating by.

Troy again tried to reply. He hurt when he tried to become alert enough to speak. Darkness again, then the voice filtered through his consciousness.

"Son, speak with me telepathically. You can. You remember, do you not?"

"Yes, yes I do, and it doesn't pain me to do so...yes, are you here dad?"

"No, not there, but I am with you now. You are in a place where I cannot be. Troy, try to open your senses. Allow yourself to become alert, aware. Tell me what you perceive."

"Darkness, warmth, safety. I feel safe here."

"Anything more? Sounds, sensations? Other than our communication, what more do your senses tell you now, son?"

"Nothing. No, wait a minute. Dad, do you hear that sound?"

"What sound, son? I hear only your voice. Concentrate on that sound. Is it neutral or does it portray danger to you? Decide quickly and act as you must," his father's voice urged.

"Pain! Head pain!" Troy's subconscious screamed out.

"Breathe through the pain and open your senses to what is around you. Evaluate the situation as you have been taught. Breathe through the pain and evaluate, Troy. You can call to Ben telepathically. You must contact Central Command," his father's voice urged.

"Yes, I must make contact," Troy breathed slowly but deeply. Antiseptic smells assailed his senses and the pain in his head lessened.

"Good, you are more alert. Troy, I must leave now. We will speak again soon. Contact Ben."

"Dad, don't go," Troy spoke aloud, but his father's voice in his mind was gone. Feeling weak, shaky and still in pain, Troy felt like weeping. How he missed the man who was his father! He tried to reach up and wipe the tears he felt on his cheek when he heard a faint rustle and the soft breath of someone beside him.

"Ah, you are awake again. Here, let me wipe your face with this damp cloth. It will feel good."

He tried to sit up but slumped to the side. "Where am it? Where did my father go?" Troy muttered.

"No, lay back, relax. You are in the hospital in Powell River. Your father is not here. Did you just dream of him?"

"No, he…I…," Troy lay back, trying to make sense of what he was feeling and of the strange situation he found himself in. He suddenly raised his head and glanced around frantically. "Brad…my shipmate, is he here too? Is he well? He had a bad infection, I remember now. Is he healing? Did I get an infection as well?"

The female smiled and said, "Oh my, you really are alert now. Good, would you like a sip of water?"

Troy realized he was parched, his throat and mouth very dry. "Yes, please."

"Oh, and he is polite too." She poured water from a pitcher into a cup with a round hollow tube in it. She brought the cup close to his face and touched his lips to one end of the tube. "Here you go. Sip slowly. Your buddy, Brad, is still feverish but conscious and doing well. I'll let him know you are awake, shall I?"

"Yes, please do," Troy replied with a groan.

"Head still throbbing?" Troy tried to nod but a flash of pain halted his movement.

"Easy now, I will give you some more medication for the pain. Just relax."

She returned and gave him two small white pills to swallow. As the pain eased, she patted his arm gently, "You will feel better in the morning."

***

The next day, when the doctor arrived, Troy was feeling much better. Though he still needed pain medication for the headache, he'd been up to the bathroom and had eaten a light breakfast of orange juice, coffee and a muffin. These were all new taste sensations, but he ate them slowly and they seemed to react well with his body. The nurse said that he had been unconscious for over 48 hours, and he couldn't remember the last time he had consumed a nutritional capsule.

"Hello, young man," a petite, gray-haired woman with a distinct English accent, said as she entered his room. "I am Dr. Janet Leas. You have been my patient since you were brought here last Friday. How are you feeling now?"

Troy smiled to himself. Ah, a human with the same accent as Cee! Interesting. "I seem to be doing well. What were my injuries?"

"You had a severe concussion from not only one, but two, strong hits to your head. From what we could see on the x-ray, it would seem you took a hit to the right-side temple area about a week ago, and a good strike to the back of the skull more recently. Your bones are knitting amazingly well, and you are in fine shape otherwise."

"Cee always does say I have a hard head," Troy quipped.

The doctor chuckled, "Well, it would seem that 'C' is correct, whoever that is?"

Troy ignored her inquiry and asked about Brad.

"Your shipmate is doing well also, but let's do some tests here first, then you may be able to visit him later. Now, lay back and open your eyes wide. The light may hurt a bit, but I need to evaluate your responses."

Troy complied.

"Well, you are on the mend, yes," the doctor said as she pulled up a chair to sit beside him. "Now, tell me what you remember."

'Uh-oh,' Troy thought, 'this is going to be tricky. I really don't remember it all, and Brad and I need to correlate our back-stories before we tell them too much.'

Dr. Leas noted his hesitation. "The yacht crew who picked you up found only a passport and some Canadian cash on your persons. The document says your name is Troy Gillis and that your last stop before entering Canadian waters was somewhere in South Africa. Does that trigger any memories?"

'Ah,' he thought, 'she is trying to determine if I have any memory loss from the injury.' Aloud, he said, "Yes, my name is Troy Gillis. I'm not sure how we got here to...Canada. I remember being stranded on an uninhabited beach and that Brad was seriously ill, and I needed to get him to medical care. I hailed the yacht, and their crew brought us on board. The next thing I remember is waking up here."

Dr. Leas eyed him carefully. "Because of the circumstances of your rescue, I needed to inform the RCMP. An officer will be by later to question you. You may have some short-term memory loss from your injuries, though I doubt this loss will be permanent. Don't try to force the memories. A chat with your friend may help trigger some of what is missing now."

"Yes, thank you. Do you know if the yacht crew found any other items on us or in our watercraft? Like my PACD? That may help shed some light on our situation," Troy said.

"What pact?" she asked looking puzzled.

Troy smiled and said, "Our Personal Auditory Communications Devices. We all wear them when on a...when at sea."

"Oh yes," she acknowledged with a smile, "the device we had to remove from your ear before giving an x-ray. The device that kept reminding you, 'Troy, call the commander, you must report to Central Command', in a voice that reminded me of my grandfather's butler in England," she said, mimicking Cee exactly.

Troy burst out laughing. "Yes, that would be Cee! Do you still have the device?"

"It should be in the bag with your personal effects. I will get the nurse to retrieve the bag for you. Maybe communicating that way will also help trigger your memory. Rest now Troy and call the nurses if you need anything. I'll be checking in with Brad now, and I will see you again later today." She stood up to move away then turned back with a mischievous grin. "I'd like to meet 'C' one day."

Troy grinned back. Just visualizing a meeting between Cee and this older petite female doctor made him chuckle. He dozed off for a time, then was awoken by a nurse bringing more food and a new bag of fluids to attach to the intravenous line in his arm.

"Eat up, Troy. How's the pain in your head?" she asked, peering down at him after affixing the new bag of fluid.

"Not too bad," he replied.

"Sure," she said sarcastically, "quite painful I'd guess by the way you're wincing and squinting. Are you nauseous at all?"

"A little," Troy admitted.

She peered at him over her glasses, "Men! You don't have to be so macho about this, you know. We all know you must be in a lot of distress after that crack on the head. Eat your meal slowly and I will bring you medication for pain so you can rest well after dinner."

The meal was again strange to him - mainly fluid, which his body seemed to accept when he sipped slowly. He barely heard the nurse when she returned.

***

Later that day, a nurse wheeled Brad into the room on a mobile chair, raised the head of Troy's bed so he could sit and left them alone to chat. Whispering, they compared their observations and began to piece together what must have happened in the last week or so. Brad had been in and out of consciousness for a few days. Troy had discussed Brad's symptoms with the Xernex medical team, and they concluded he must have contracted some sort of systemic infection and would need antibiotic treatment, which they did not have on board their landing craft. They suggested using the submersible to transfer Brad to a medical facility on land nearby. Troy could not remember much from that point on.

"I don't recall a lot either. What could have happened between you getting me into the submersible and our rescue?" Brad wondered.

"Brad, do you have your PACD?"

"No, I don't know what became of that either!"

"Doctor Leas said they had removed mine prior to doing some x-rays on my head, and it was probably in a bag with other personal items we had on arrival. You may want to ask about that too."

Troy told Brad about how the doctor had heard the device asking him to call the commander, and how she had said she would like to meet Cee. Brad's eyes widened in disbelief. "Oh, I think not! Can you just see Cee tangling with that feisty petite woman?"

"Oh, can't you visualize the two of them dancing together, Cee and Dr. Leas," Troy quipped. "They are about the same height and speak the same language."

Both men were having a good laugh at that image when Kevin Warden and another man walked into the room. "It sounds like you two are feeling a lot better," Kevin commented. "I'd like you two to meet my father, Wayne Warden. Dad, meet Troy Gillis and his buddy, Brad...?"

"Bradley Sykes," Brad replied, "pleased to meet you, sir. And thank you, Kevin, for rescuing us when you did."

"I'm glad we found you before the storm hit. It was a bad one and did a lot of damage along the west coastline," Kevin replied.

The men chatted a bit. Wayne was eyeing Troy carefully all the while. “So, young man, just who are you? There certainly is a familial resemblance between us, but I don’t remember hearing of a long lost relative. What were you two doing in Canadian coastal waters without decent ID, eh?” Wayne leaned forward, watching Troy carefully as he spoke.

“Now, dad...” Kevin began.

Wayne put up his hand to stop Kevin. “Let the young man speak. I’d like to hear what he has to say for himself.”

‘Oh-oh here we go,’ Troy thought. He glanced surreptitiously at Brad, who gave him a faint nod. “Our names are as is stated on our passports. I have very little recall of what has happened over the last few days, and Brad has been in and out of consciousness for about a week. I know that the decision was made that I load Brad into the submersible and get him to a medical facility on land as soon as possible. That is what I did.”

“Brad, while you were unconscious, you mumbled about a fire…blaze, you said. Could there have been a fire aboard do you think, or was it merely that you were so feverish?” Kevin asked.

Brad shrugged, “I don’t recall. I wish I could. This is very frustrating.”

“The doctor said that Coast Guard officers would also be questioning our presence here,” Troy commented. “I’m sure we both have proper identification aboard Xer…our mothership, and we will contact them as soon as the staff here returns our PACDs…Personal Auditory Communication Devices...that we use while at sea.”

Brad’s nurse appeared just then and said, “I’ll bet you are a feeling a bit weary by now. I’ll take you back to your room.”

Brad nodded to her. "Nice to have met you two," he said to Kevin and Wayne, and the nurse wheeled him out of the room.

Troy turned to the penetrating gaze of Wayne Warden, who said, "You are very young to be in command of a ship."

'Are all humans so skeptical?' he wondered tiredly. "When we are on a mission aboard the landing craft, I am designated commander, but I report to the commander on Xernex, our mothership. Brad's specialty is marine biology, and mine is marine architecture," Troy mumbled.

Wayne stood. "You must be tired; you're not making any sense. We will return later, if we may."

"Yes, please do," Troy replied weakly as he lay back on the pillow. He really was tired, and his head was throbbing.

Dr. Leas arrived later in the evening with a plastic bag with a drawstring containing his personal items, including the PACD. "I hear you overtired yourself with company earlier," she admonished. "Troy, you are recovering well, but you need to rest more. Rest is your best medicine now and don't hesitate to call for pain medication if you need it."

He nodded his agreement.

"On that note, I have been asked to tell you that an RCMP officer will be here to talk with you and Brad in the morning. I don't want either of you to worry about this. It's normal procedure in cases where folks mysteriously land up on our shores," she said with a grin.

"Thank you, now that I have my PACD I can contact Cee and get this cleared up," Troy replied.

Dr. Leas patted his leg and said, “Good, rest now.” Then, as she was walking out of the room, she turned the lights down low and pulled the door shut.

Kevin and Wayne arrived shortly after Troy had consumed another meal, and he was feeling somewhat stronger.

“Kevin, where is our submersible?” Troy asked.

“In my father-in-law’s boathouse on Savary Island, why?”

“First, I would request that he, or someone you trust, go inside and check for any documentation we may have left there. An RCMP officer will be by tomorrow and any further paperwork to verify our identities would be helpful. Secondly, as you have noted, our two-man submersible is…rather unique.”

“I’ll say it is! Dad, you need to see this watercraft,” Kevin enthused.

“Yes, well it is a prototype that we have developed and are testing. We need to keep it secret for now. Competition in the field of marine architecture is fierce, and we don’t want our competitors knowing about this design yet. So, I would like to keep it hidden for now. Can you do that?” Troy asked, keeping to their back-story script and hoped he could trust these men.

Kevin glanced at his father, who nodded. “Yes, we can do that. I’ll ask John to check it out, see if he can find any more ID for you two, and keep the machine under wraps for now. But I can tell you, once that machine is authorized, I have no doubt the marine sciences department at UBC will want a look at it, too.”

Troy grinned and said, “We’ll see what we can do for you later. Thanks for assisting us now.”

Chapter 10

By the time the RCMP officers arrived the next morning, both Brad and Troy had contacted Cee; they had synchronized their back-story with as much of what had occurred in the last few days as they could remember. The older officer had been very skeptical, the younger one more accommodating. It was agreed that they would not be jailed; "Yet!" the older man had stated forcefully. They were not to leave the area either once they got out of hospital. The RCMP would check out their story and would probably want to see them again, as would the Coast Guard.

"Well, that wasn't too bad, as far as interrogations go!" Brad stated when he entered Troy's room later.

"Yes, I'd say it went well. I asked Kevin to check our equipment and other areas on the sub to see if they can find more documentation. I am sure there is more, either on the sub or on our landing craft, and we need to find it before the Coast Guard interview tomorrow."

Brad agreed and added, "And you could contact Cee again and have him check with Mission Control, but how do we get the information here? Our communication band isn't compatible with any here on land."

"We'll deal with that tomorrow," Troy said with a tired sigh. "Should we let the Coast Guard know about our little episode with the stranded whale?"

Brad laughed, "Troy, you are already a hero and being touted as another 'dolphin-speaker like Kevin' to many here. I'm sure they've heard the story or soon will."

"I'm no hero. We just did what was needed in the moment," Troy stated.

"Uh-huh."

"Dismissed," Troy growled at Brad.

"Aye, aye, sir," Brad replied with a mocking salute, chuckling as he wheeled himself back to his room.

Later the next morning, Fritz and Kevin returned with the materials they had found on the submersible. Wayne handed Troy the two long, flat, soft containers they had found in the sleeves of the men's aquatic gear. Inside was the documentation they needed, as well as access to the local bank.

"Thank you. These will help clarify some questions the police and Coast Guard may have," Troy said.

"You may want to hide these…if you are not licenced to carry dangerous weapons. These look mighty lethal to me," Fritz said, handing over the soft metallic case that housed their quistyrs.

Brad chuckled and explained about the quistyrs being presented to young people when they reached the age of majority, as an honor and a right-of-passage. "Each quistyr has the emblem of its recipient's date of birth, and personal familial logo or design. They are highly prized and utile as well - see how the one edge annealed with diamond dust to give it a strong, but serrated edge."

"Impressive," Wayne agreed, "but dangerous."

"It can be if needs be," Troy agreed calmly, then turned to Kevin. "We will be let out of the hospital soon, and we will need some sort of on-land lodgings for a time until we recuperate and repair our sub."

Kevin said, "Yes, dad and I have discussed this. John, Fritz and I will need to head back to Vancouver tomorrow, but dad and his friends, as well as Jack Kern from the Coast Guard, will help you get settled here in Powell River for a while. I hope that I can see the two of you before you move on."

"We'll contact you whenever we are in Vancouver," assured Brad.

Chapter 11

Troy and Brad were discharged from hospital, and as promised, Wayne and his friends found lodging for them in a small motel along Marine Drive, just up from the Powell River Marina. Sara, Kevin's mother, had even thought to send a set of clothing for each man. On the way from the hospital to the motel, Wayne pointed out some of the local attractions.

"Marine Drive runs along the waterfront and is the main road from the ferry terminal at Earl's Cove to the northern tip of the peninsula, the wharf at Lund. You will find most everything you need within walking distance of the motel," Wayne commented. "Banks, cafes, shops, and a small grocer are just a couple of blocks up from the marina. Well, here we are," he said as he turned in and parked in front of the office of a clean, cedar log cabin styled motel.

"Uh, how much does the room cost? Brad and I thought that in pooling our Canadian funds we could perhaps rent the place for a week, or at least until we can get to a bank. Living aboard ship, as we do, we seldom have to concern ourselves with currency exchanges," Troy commented ruefully.

Wayne raised an eyebrow and said, "From what I saw, you two have sufficient funds for a while, but there is a bank two blocks north of here if you need it. Just sign the registry and hand Gerta a few of your hundred-dollar bills and you will be set."

Once inside the small motel office, Wayne introduced Troy and Brad to the manager, Gerta. They signed the registry, gave Gerta four hundred dollars, and she gave them each a key to their room. It would all have been quite exciting if for Troy if he had not been so very tired. Wayne seemed to understand his fatigue and left as soon as the men had settled into the motel room. They quickly explored the area: a small sitting area, two good-sized beds, a galley and a head.

"On-land dwellings have different names than our water-crafts," Brad reminded Troy. "Here, we have a kitchen and a bathroom; and I think these beds will be much more comfortable than our bunks on Xernex." He laid down with a pleasurable moan, pulled a blanket over himself, and promptly started to snore.

Troy chuckled and reported to Cee, "We have secured a small on-land abode that seems safe and secure. Let Syvers know that I will be calling in again as soon as I've rested." He gave Cee the pertinent coordinates, locked the only door and snuggled into his own bed.

For the next two days, they mainly rested, watched news and other programs on the television and walked over to the café for regular meals. They quickly caught on to the monetary system in Canada and met a few of the locals at the café. To Troy's surprise, it seemed several folks had already heard of him and Brad from an article in the local newspaper about their episode with the whale, and about their own dramatic rescue before the storm. As well, Jack Kern from the Coast Guard had called to arrange a time for an official interview to complete their naval incident report.

***

"That interview went well," Brad commented after the two Coast Guard officers left. "The older fellow, Chuck, is certainly more skeptical of us, but Jack seemed to buy our story."

"Agreed, but we really do not remember a lot about what a happened before the rescue, so you can't blame him for being dubious. If only I could recall more. Here I am with a near photographic memory, supposedly, but it's all a blank," Troy complained.

"Troy, don't fret about it," Brad counselled. "We gave them the coordinates for the area where we rescued the whale, and for that garbage dump near our landing site. Both men seemed quite interested in that, and they will, I think, follow up getting help to clean up the area. That's a positive! That's what we are here to accomplish after all, right?"

"Besides," Brad continued to say, "as Dr. Leas said, seeing the submersible again on Monday when you and Wayne go over to Savary Island with the Coast Guard, may just trigger some of that elusive memory. I wish I could go with you, but alas the good doctor needs to run more tests on me that morning."

"Oh, and I do believe I overheard you planning to meet with the waitress at the cafe, Marge, before her shift that afternoon," Troy teased.

"Ah yes," Brad said leaning back in his chair with a smug grin and a twinkle in his eye, "a very good-looking, interesting woman she is."

"Brad, are you sure it's a good idea to get romantically involved with a human? We are not going to be here that long, after all," Troy commented lightly.

"Aye, captain," he replied with a mock salute, "I'm just getting to know the locals. Checking out the territory, as they say."

Troy laughed, "You're incorrigible!"

Chapter 12

The day was warm and sunny as Wayne drove Troy out to Lund where, he was told, they would board the Coast Guard vessel and sail to Savary Island. They were going to find their submersible that was hidden under a tarp beneath the deck of John's cabin. Troy still had some trepidation about letting the others view the craft, but according to Wayne, each of the crew had signed a non-disclosure agreement on the pretext of this being an experimental vessel. Central Command had approved this venture, so Troy tried to relax and enjoy the ride to Lund. He said, "This really is a beautiful area. Our commander aboard Xernex has agreed to give us a few weeks to recuperate, so Brad and I would like to do a bit of touring before we get back to work."

"Good idea," Wayne agreed; "rent a car and travel south along the coast or take a ferry over to Vancouver Island. There is much to see here. Do either of you have a Canadian Driver's License?"

'Oh-oh, this could be tricky,' Troy thought. "Well, no, but I have a European driving certificate from when I studied languages there," he lied. "Will that do?"

Wayne laughed and said, “Temporarily maybe, but you will need to get a Canadian one if you plan to stay around here.”

They drove on in silence as Troy admired the tall trees, lush forest undergrowth and birds along the side of the winding road.

“Here we are,” Wayne cried, as they swung around the final bend and down toward the Lund Wharf. “The Coast Guard Cutter is waiting.”

Introductions were made again after the two men had boarded the cutter. Troy remembered Jack and Chuck. A younger man named Rick and a paramedic, Anna, had joined the crew for this outing. “Has everyone signed a non-disclosure?” Wayne asked. “The vessel you are about to see is a prototype built by our friend, Troy, here. Because of the, sometimes-fierce, competition in the field of marine architecture, his company has asked we keep all knowledge of this craft secret while Troy and Brad run trials in these waters, even as they conduct studies and document the oceanic pollution problems along our coast.”

“Yes, we all understand this, Wayne. And in return, you have permission to share any findings, regarding the pollution problem here, with us...correct?” Chuck said gruffly.

“Yes,” Troy replied.

The Cutter moored along the dock below the cabin. Once the tarp was removed revealing the submersible there was an audible collective gasp.

“Wow,” Rick exclaimed as he circled the craft, “just how fast can this baby go and how deep?”

“Is that glass? No, it’s not glass. What is this thing made of?” Anna murmured as she ran her hands along the upper walls.

Troy smiled to himself, seeing it again as if for the first time. Yes, it was certainly something they had not seen before. Cigar-shaped, with two seats sitting back-to-back within a clear glass-like structure, and with instrument panels at fore and aft, the sub was easily maneuverable and allowed maximum visibility.

"It is self-contained, and it can be utilized above or below water level. We are still putting it through trials so are not sure as to how much speed or depth we can attain with this prototype. That is part of the trials we are conducting here in the cooler waters of the north Pacific Ocean," Troy prevaricated, while he proceeded to study the exterior in depth, trying to figure out what had occurred on his last run.

"What do you make of these markings on the cowling?" Jack asked.

Troy moved closer. "I'm not sure. We were not close enough to shore to encounter shore flora or sea grasses, I don't think, until we ran aground. Damn, I wish I could remember!" Moving around the craft, he ran his fingers along the surface near the area by his chair.

"Here," Troy exclaimed, "could this be the reason for my shoulder's injury?"

Jack and Chuck rushed over.

"Yeah, looks like a bullet hole, all right, penetrated the exterior too," Chuck agreed. "Come take some pictures of this, Rick, and take some of those striations on the cowling as well."

Troy moved along, checking his craft carefully. "Ahh," he cried suddenly and grabbed at the edge, trying not to collapse as pain shot through his head.

Jack glanced over then yelled, "Anna, bring your kit. Chuck, help me get Troy up on the deck. Dr. Leas was afraid this could happen. Troy, let's get you up on a chair on deck."

Troy moaned and clutched his head.

Once they had a helped him to a deck chair, Anna gave him a glass of water and an analgesic for his headache. "Just lean back and relax Troy," she advised. "We will chat later."

Troy did just that; he leaned back, closed his eyes, tried to breathe easily, and tried to relax. The pain eased after a bit, and he sat up and opened his eyes to see Jack watching him carefully.

"A break-through?" Jack asked.

"Yes," Troy shuddered and continued in a shaky voice, "before it was all a blank, but now it's in disturbing living color. Yes, I remember it all."

"Good, just take it slowly. Do you mind if I record our conversation? Chuck will want to hear it later."

"That's okay," Troy said then hesitated, trying to regroup his thoughts, as Jack watched him closely.

"You told us Brad had been very ill and that the medics aboard the Xernex suggested you get him to hospital, right?" Jack prompted.

"Yes, that's right, Jack. The bad gash Brad had sustained to his thigh while we were freeing that whale became infected, and he was delirious with fever. I determined that the closest medical facility was in Tofino, so after getting him settled in the submersible, I set course for that town. We were skimming close to the surface to avoid any underwater surprises, and since I had not seen any other craft nearby, I was racing full throttle toward land. Brad was still very feverish and slipping in and out of consciousness."

Troy stopped speaking for a moment, bent forward as if in pain, then straightened and gazed off into the distance, remembering. He continued, "Suddenly the area around us became murky and teeming with sea life. Fish of all kinds crammed together, tumbling and bumping into the craft. I slowed the rotors, trying to avoid the fish. Then we too seemed to twist and tumble with the crowd. Brad was thrown to one side, against the window. I tried to gain control of our craft, but it too was being swept along with the others. The craft held power, but the navigational devices were compromised. I realized I needed to surface to get my bearings, but which way was up?"

Troy groaned and shuddered again, took a sip of water, and continued his narrative. "Then, through the murky waters, I spied an opening where light was filtering from above. We were all in a boundary of netting, like the material we had to cut from the whale we rescued. I remember thinking, 'if I can break though that net and reach the surface, we will be okay.' It took a few tries, but eventually we broke through the netting. That is probably how the cowling got scraped."

Troy glanced at Chuck, who had joined them on the deck.

"With fish swarming all around us, we escaped. When we surfaced, I spotted a large vessel to what I thought to be north of our earlier position. As we neared land that I thought was the western reaches of Vancouver Island, I realized I needed to rethink my plan. I remembered spotting several larger human centers on the leeward side of the island, so I decided to try for them, rather than heading back south to Tofino."

Chuck, Anna, and Jack sat together quietly and listened carefully, with growing concern on their faces, as Troy continued, "Two single-man speedboats raced toward us from the larger vessel I had seen. I assumed they were friendly, so I slowed, thinking to ask for help. They did not respond to my international distress signal but came along-side and fired upon us. Shocked, I immediately angled the sub into a deep dive, but as the navigational equipment was still inoperative, I needed to surface again to get my bearings. I had not seen the speed boats while underwater, but they were upon us shortly after we surfaced. We were closer to land now, so I decided to outrun them. Dodging small land masses and other craft in the area, diving and surfacing again, racing around the northern tip of the island, I eventually ran us aground. Those two men were still in pursuit. After making sure Brad was breathing and as comfortable as possible, I left him in the sub, removed the headgear from my aquatic suit, and confronted the men with my quistyr hidden but at the ready."

"Now, I know several languages," Troy said, "but I did not understand what it was they were yelling at me. They were obviously very angry. One was waving a large gun; the other held a club of some sort. Then they must have seen John's vessel, or the ruckus of the dolphins milling about in the bay distracted them, for one rushed forward and struck me a sharp blow to the head before they raced away. I collapsed on the sand and the rest you know."

Wayne, Rick and the rest of the crew had heard Troy's story as well. They sat in silence. Then, Chuck asked Troy if he could describe the men who had pursued him.

"They wore aquatic gear and helmets, so no, I could not tell you much. Both men were shorter in stature than myself, but I assume they were male by their walk and stance. Their language had a sing-song cadence like some Eastern cultures do, but I could not identify it. I called their crafts speedboats because they are swift, though not as fast as our submersible."

"Describe the speedboats," suggested Wayne.

"Cigar-shaped, open, about the size of a large motorcycle with a rear outboard motor," Troy said with his eyes closed as he remembered.

"Any distinctive markings?" asked Rick.

"No, they were dull grey or blue grey in color; they blended well into the surrounding environment. I remember they were noisy as they approached. I heard them before I saw them."

"Could you give us an idea as to where you were when they first fired upon you?" Chuck asked.

"I can get the latest coordinates from Cee, because until I'd lost navigational power, I reported in at regular intervals."

Using his PACD, Troy communicated with Cee and obtained the required information. "Oh, and Cee, could you give me the coordinates for the area where we last collected specimens?"

"Certainly, sir."

Troy turned to Jack and said, "Shortly before Brad became too ill, we were exploring a ridge to the south of our berth. We both felt it was a large garbage dumping site."

"If you can get that information for us, we will investigate it," Chuck said, then he continued, "You have certainly given us some incredibly good leads and a lot of work to do, young man.

We do appreciate your and your company's cooperation. Is there anything we can help you with now?"

Troy sighed and said with a grin, "Get me home, so I can rest a bit. But seriously, Brad and I have been looking for an on-land base where we can repair our crafts before continuing our mission. We plan to rent a small yacht to tour around. We need a dock and boat shed in a secluded area."

Jack glanced at Wayne then said, "I think we could find you something nearby. Leave that to us. Now young man, let's get you back to your motel."

Troy was exhausted by the time he returned to the motel. Brad was still out, so he flopped into bed for a quick snooze.

"Hey Troy, it's supper time. Wake up! I want to hear all," Brad exclaimed, shaking the man's shoulder gently.

Troy sat up slowly, still feeling groggy and a bit dazed. Brad watched him closely.

"You remembered, didn't you?"

Troy nodded and said, "I did, just as Dr. Leas thought I might. I'll clean up a bit and then let's get some food. I'll tell you everything over a meal.

Jack called to let the men know that he had found a possible on-land site for them. "It's an old, abandoned logging camp north of here, near Desolation Sound Marine Park. There is a long dock and a good-sized boat shed. But...," Jack warned, "the place could need some repairs. I've not been by there in a while, and it's been abandoned for years now."

Jack and Troy discussed the possibility of renting the old logging camp; it seemed a perfect match for their needs. They agreed to meet at the Lund Marina the following Monday to run out and look at it.

Chapter 13

Brad and Troy anchored their small, rented yacht at the marina, then they boarded the Coast Guard vessel for the trip to Desolation Sound. Once on-board, Troy introduced Brad to the crew.

"So, what have you to been doing lately?" Jake asked.

"We rented a boat and have been playing tourist for the most part," Troy replied.

"This coast really is a lovely spot. I'm glad we got to see a part of it and meet more of the locals," Brad commented. "But if this old logging camp you mentioned is available, and suited to our needs, well, it will be good to get back to work again!"

"Yes, and Cee is getting lonely sitting out there in the launch craft in the middle of nowhere by himself," Troy added with a chuckle. Brad laughed, enjoying the fact that Jake and the others did not know Cee was a robot.

"We are heading into the deeper waters of Desolation Sound Marine Park now. Our destination is an old logging operation on the western edge of the park, about sixteen nautical miles from Powell River," Hank told the men. "No one has logged the area in years, but it does have a long wharf and a large boat shed.

Both need repair, but not so much that a few boards, nails, and hard work can't fix."

"If you two find this location to be suitable, we will arrange for you to negotiate with the son of the owner to lease this space for the winter," Jake added.

"It sounds to be worth looking at. Our own search for a spot hasn't been too successful so far," Brad said.

"Here we are," Chuck commented.

Scanning the shore, Troy saw nothing but a rugged coastline strewn with rotting logs and other debris, clogged with tall trees and thick underbrush. Not much by way of civilization, but that was good for them. "The water looks to be suitably deep here," he said.

"But the place isn't much to look at," Jack said with a chuckle. "Why don't we dock over there and have a good look around before you decide."

"Be careful! The dock isn't in the best repair. We found a pile of lumber stacked on the back porch of the house that sits further in the bush. There is enough wood there to start mending the dock," Chuck informed them. "You will need to clear away some of the brush on land and along the shore. If you want privacy, it may be best to leave the area as wild as is workable for you - less obvious that way."

"The dock and boat shed need some repair, but if you want to use the house you are looking at doing some major renovations. It's up to you how much or how little you need," Jack added.

The men tramped around the area making note of what was offered and what would be needed.

"Yes, I think we could make this work. Brad, what do you think?" Troy asked.

"Seems alright to me, captain," Brad replied smugly, "but you need to get the launch craft here quickly; we can put Cee to work cleaning up around here."

Back onboard the Coast Guard vessel, Chuck placed a call to the owner's son in Vancouver. Chuck clued him in and introduced him to Troy and Brad.

"I'll be in Powell River this coming weekend. We could meet then. Meanwhile, I will chat with my father, who is presently vacationing in Florida, and discuss this with him. You say you would like to rent the place for the fall and winter months, correct?"

"Yes, that works for us," Brad replied, "but when figuring the rent, you need to consider that we will have to do major cleanup and repairs before the place is livable."

"I'm sure we will be able to come to an amiable agreement," the man replied smoothly. "I will see you on the weekend. Go ahead and start clearing brush in the meantime, if you like."

Brad dusted his hands together gleefully, saying, "Well, that seems like a go, right captain? Now we can get to work!"

"Yes," Troy replied thoughtfully, "we will need equipment to clear away the brush, as well as tools like hammers and saws. I suppose we could find a place in Powell River to rent these, right? How do we dispose of the waste and debris?"

Jack chuckled and said, "Oh, in Powell River, being a harbor town that it is, you will find plenty of hardware stores, both privately owned and chain stores like Rona. There are several right on Marine Drive. Boaters are notorious for being self-helpers."

"And since it's later in the season now, we are not likely to issue fire bans, so you can just pile up the brush and debris on the beach and burn it at low tide," Chuck informed the men.

"Troy, have you had a chance to check out the electronics and navigational systems on the sub? We have several well-stocked electronics shops in the Westview area. If they don't have what you need, you may want to drop into the boat builder you passed on the way to Lund. They manufacture very sophisticated yachts, so they may be able to help you."

"Thank you, Jake. I may have to check that out," Troy agreed.

Chapter 14

Two weeks later, Troy and Brad had cleared a good-sized area, had hired a builder to extend the boatshed to nearly the end of the dock, and they left the roof of that section open for maximum sunlight. Brad and Troy had done the underwater work necessary for the extension, as to the builders' suggestions, and it had worked out well. Troy had repaired the sub and taken it out at night on several trial runs. Now, seated on the dock in deck chairs they had recently purchased in Powell River, Brad sighed contentedly. "We landed on earth just over a month ago, and look what we have accomplished so far," he commented while gesturing lazily around.

"Yes, I think the commander will be pleased with our progress," Troy replied. "It has been a pleasure interacting with planet Earth and her people. Just look at that amazing sunset! We don't get those on Fentanys. This really is a picturesque place."

Brad agreed, saying, "Yes, having two suns as we do on Fentanys means we seldom see true sunsets, right? So, this view is a treat to behold."

"The people we have met so far are most kind, don't you think? But when listening to their newscasts and reading their newspapers, it appears that human beings here are not as evolved as the inhabitants of Fentanys or other galaxies we have seen and learned about," Troy mused pensively.

"What do you mean, Troy?" Brad asked, sitting forward more attentively.

Troy took a moment to think, then he said, "The individuals we have met so far are kind and helpful, and I truly do admire their concepts of family, of caring, of sharing and of loyalty. But, when you listen to their newscasts and read the papers - if what we are hearing and reading is truth - well, humans don't seem to understand yet that for their species to survive, they must learn to appreciate and respect this planet on which they live and to live in harmony with Earth and with one another. It's sad really. Earth is one of the lushest and most verdant of the planets we have studied and seen; it offers everything humans need for survival, but they do not appreciate it or each other."

Brad glanced at Troy and chuckled. "Getting a bit philosophical, aren't you? What brought that on?"

Troy shrugged, "Just an observation."

"Well, enough ruminating. I think it's time we got back to work," Brad stated.

"I agree, let's leave just after dark. We can head north to open waters and take the submersible through a few more test runs in deep diving and aerials, then we can get to our launch craft by early morning. Cee will be glad to see us, I think."

"True," Brad replied with a chuckle, "and we need to have direct contact with Xernex. I wonder if we will be allowed to contact Raj and Maria yet, to see how they are faring."

"Yes, I'll certainly ask about that, and if Ben has had any communication with my father as well."

***

They reached their launch craft and docked without a problem. Then, later that night, they checked in with the Xernex crew and slept well in their own comfortable berths.

"Let's check the flora and fauna in this area once more before heading out to the Desolation Sound area," Brad suggested.

"Good idea, I would like to check out the area near that dumpsite we spotted earlier. Jake seemed suspicious of what may be happening there. It's outside Canadian territorial waters, therefore problematic if something illegal or dangerous is occurring there."

They suited up in their aquatic gear, attached tethering lines and set out a short time later. The sea was calm, and the sun was warm. It was not long before a group of dolphins appeared but kept at a distance, watching. Troy enjoyed the sensation of being in deep water again, the ease of movement, the buoyancy, the welcoming of Earth's inhabitants. 'We've had a successful sojourn here on earth so far,' Troy thought happily, as they leisurely crested the ridge they had explored before. 'I trust Ben is pleased with our observations.'

Brad's voice sliced through Troy's musings. "Would you look at that. What a mess!" Brad exclaimed pointing down at a narrow valley. It was a mess indeed! Jettisoned barrels, plastics, even what looked to be old furniture and metallic tubing, and masses of that mesh that so entangled the fish here, littered the ocean floor. What a waste, what a hazard! “This is still outside Jake’s authority I think, but let’s let him know anyway,” Brad suggested.

“Agreed, but I’d like to check the area to the east past this mess and over that next low ridge. There seems to be a low vibration coming from there.”

“Yes,” Brad said, “I sensed that too. Let’s check it out then report in.”

Underwater turbulence increased and the noise level with it as they neared the top of the ridge. Fish were conspicuously absent from the area. Then they spotted it - a huge ship with diesel engines throbbing, belching waste products and debris.

“Yuck,” Brad cried, “this is probably the reason for that mess, and now they are making another one! I have the coordinates of both.”

“Good, let’s get back and report,” Troy communicated. “At least the fish have the sense to stay clear, but the damage to the ocean flora will be tremendous. What a tragedy! I wish we could do more than just observe.”

Back onboard, Brad rechecked their craft’s exterior then he and Cee prepared it for take-off while Troy spoke with his supervisor, Syvers, about what they had observed. He was given permission to share their findings with the local authorities. “From the information we have, it would appear that the vessel is only two or three nautical miles from the Canadian coastal boundary,” Troy pointed out. “I thought that with your permission we could, uh, encourage that vessel to move further toward land. That way, the Canadian Coast Guard could board it and evaluate what is happening there."

"I see," Syvers said with a chuckle. "Your mission is getting a bit boring, and you want to create some excitement. Your Earth mission is one of observation only, remember."

"Well...," Troy began.

"Perhaps a bit of harassment in order to drive the vessel eastward would be permissible, but no flaming or destruction of any kind," he admonished.

"I've not discussed this with Brad yet, but I thought we'd rise from the ocean and approach from the west. Our launch craft is much larger than their vessel, and with the setting sun behind us, we would be indistinct but viably threatening. A few passes should encourage them to haul anchor and move east. What do you think?" Troy entreated.

With another chuckle, Syvers said, "Not a bad plan, but Troy, you need to be careful not to draw undue attention to yourselves and at no time cause them to need to retaliate, understood? And report back immediately upon your return to base."

"Yes sir, thank you sir," Troy said and concluded the transmission.

"Oh yes, let's give those nasty folks a little scare!" Brad agreed when Troy outlined his plan. Brad's eyes sparkled with anticipation and a little mischief as he leaned forward, clasping his fist under his chin. "Okay no flaming, but how about we flash them with strobe lights or some high-frequency sound just to annoy them? What fun!"

Troy grinned and said, "Looking for a bit of excitement, are you? That's what Syvers accused me of as well. Yes, we can harass them a bit but are to remain discreet and not invoke a negative reaction. I think we could encourage them to move closer inland if we maneuver carefully."

"Good! Let's do it!"

Troy shared his plan: "The weather is to be favorable, so I thought to take our launch craft further out to sea, run a few arial and aquatic tests, then approach them by air after rising from the sea a few nautical miles to the west of their vessel. With the sunset behind us, we would be indistinct, but a clear threat to them if we play it right."

"Good plan, sir," Cee said, then added, "But move in silently until we are almost above them. The splash of our assent from the ocean should be enough to get their attention, as will the shadow of our approach with the sun at the aft."

"Good point, Cee," Brad agreed. "How high do you plan to fly, Troy? We need to stay out of their firing range, and we do not know the capacity of the weapons they may be carrying onboard. If they are criminals, they may be well armed."

"That's true. I'll call Jack and let him know our plan, and I'll give him the coordinates of those two dump sites," Troy replied.

***

Their launch craft, though having been idle for so long, handled beautifully in both arial and diving maneuvers. Both men were pleased with the results. As the sun sunk slowly in the west, Troy brought their craft up from a deep dive into the air above causing a mighty splash, then it rose and silently approached the vessel.

"Brad, take the coordinates of that other larger ship to the south of the one we are approaching. It looks like this one, but it is far enough away not to interfere, I hope."

"Yes, I saw that. Let's check it out on our return flight," Brad replied.

"Will do - Cee, are you picking up any radio chatter from the vessel or anything nearby?" asked Troy.

"Yes sir, but it is undecipherable."

"Record it anyway."

"Certainly, sir."

"We've been spotted!" Brad cried as their shadow slowly overtook the vessel. "Lots of activity on deck and a smaller craft is approaching from the east. Can you hover a little lower? We can get an audio from the outboard receivers. We are slowed enough so the wind from the props shouldn't interfere."

Troy responded, "Okay...descending...keep a close eye on activity...I don't want to be shot down!" Their shadow now engulfed the vessel. They could pick up some frantic shouts and points to the sky, even as the small craft approached and docked close to the larger vessel. More frantic shouting ensued, and one man was pointing a gun and firing upward, but Troy had their launch craft hovering low and to the west, so the shooter was firing into the shadow, not at them.

A large man stepped up from the smaller boat, marching angrily on deck.

"Amplify the external audio," Troy demanded.

"Stop shooting at shadows, you fuckin' idiots," he shouted in broad English, "and get me your captain now…and speak English. No English, no sale!"

A smaller person came rushing forward and spoke so faintly that the men in the launch craft could barely hear.

The bigger man yelled, "What? I was told… Don't you dare fuck with me, you goddamn chinks." Then, he screamed, "Boswell!"

Another man stepped up from the smaller boat, a large rifle at the ready. The others on board stepped forward, weapons drawn as well.

The smaller person raised a hand in a halting motion and spoke softly, gesturing for the men to stand down. Several bedraggled-looking young women were pushed out onto the deck.

Troy growled, "Human trafficking, I would say. Time for some fun. Hit the strobe-lights, Cee. Brad, alert the Coast Guard. I'm going to hover right above. We really need to stop those immoral criminals."

Troy brought their launch craft in closer, with lights flashing. Chaos erupted on the deck. The big guy and his sidekick tried to get back on the smaller boat, but Troy angled the forward thruster so the wind from it shoved the boats further apart. The young women scurried back inside, out of sight.

"There is more chatter from the other vessel, captain," C reported, "I cannot decipher it, but the tone sounds urgent."

"What are their coordinates, Brad? Get an approximate to the Coast Guard, now," Troy ordered.

Troy moved their launch craft in closer and lower, causing the wind from the rotators to push at the vessel. Then, just as he had hoped, the vessel's captain started the engines and began moving. It moved west at first, but with several deft maneuvers, Troy blocked that move, so they had to turn northeast. Another careful push by Troy, and the other vessel sped due east at full throttle. "Quickly, get those coordinates to the Coast Guard. I hope they are in place."

"The Coast Guard is three nautical miles ahead," Cee informed them.

"Good, time for us to disappear," Troy said.

"Aw, captain, can't we stay and watch the capture?" Brad whined.

Troy laughed and said, "Cut the strobe-lights, but leave the outer audio open. We will check out that other vessel now, and then we must get out of here. Sorry to spoil your fun, Brad."

Again, Troy had their launch craft approach from the west. Though the sun had nearly set, they still had the advantage of reduced visibility. This vessel was bigger and was obviously on alert, with heavier artillery mounted on the deck. Troy had to travel higher and at a greater speed to remain out of range, but they did get some good photographs of the vessel and the weapons.

"Fast moving airplane approaching to the starboard, Troy," Cee commented. "It is not Canadian Coast Guard but appears to be an official aircraft of some kind. Can we out-maneuver it, sir?"

"Certainly, thank you Cee. What's the terrain below us?"

"A high ridge directly but a deeper trench to the right. They are firing at us, sir!"

"Noted; strap into your places," Troy urged, "here we go."

Troy pushed the forward throttle quickly to maximum speed then made a sharp 90 degree right angled turn. He immediately released the throttle then plunged the craft straight into the trench. Impact was tremendous, but they managed to stay on course.

"Wow! That was amazing Troy," Brad chortled when the craft settled, and the men had caught their breaths.

"Damage?" Troy barked.

Brad did a quick survey and reported, "Nothing visible, but how about we head back? Cee hasn't yet seen our new homebase and we all need to relax after this little adventure."

Chapter 15

Jake and his wife Anna sat on the dock in deck chairs with Troy and Brad on this particularly lovely early October evening. The men and Cee had settled in after their earlier adventure, and Jake had come by to report on what had occurred because of their foray with the foreign vessels out at sea. Troy called to Cee, who was working within their launch craft, to bring out a tray of coffee and donuts, then turned to Jake saying, "We are genuinely enjoying these evenings. It's amazing the way the sun slowly sinks into the open ocean then sets with a final flare of bright green light."

"Yes," Ann agreed, "further inland, the mountains obscure this sight but…." She glanced up in surprise as Cee wafted out onto the wharf, "Is that a…a robot?" she gasped.

Troy chuckled, thoroughly enjoying Jake and Ann's reaction. "Cee, I would like you to meet Jake and Anna. Folks, we call him Cee."

"A pleasure to meet you sir, madam," Cee stated in his best old-English butler voice.

"Nice to meet you, too," Ann sputtered, reached out for a handshake, then quickly dropped her hand in embarrassment. "Cripes Jake, I think he would bow to us if a robot could bow."

"Will that be all, sir?" asked Cee.

"Yes, thank you," Troy said, then added, "Dismissed."

"Very good sir," Cee intoned, then he turned sharply and glided back up to the boat shed.

Brad let out a whoop of laughter, "Troy, how do you get him to do that English butler schtick so well? Jake, you wouldn't believe the fun we have with that little guy, nor the amazing stuff Troy has programmed the robot to do. Troy's expertise is marine architecture, but he dabbles in a lot of other sciences as well."

Troy responded, "I built Cee as an aid while we were still in training onboard Xernex. The ship's commander saw the progress I made with Cee and suggested that he may be of use on these expeditions. The other two landing parties out there have trained robots on board as well. Like the subs, these robots are prototypes and are being tested and perfected as we go along."

"Can you make me one, Troy?" Anna asked with a cheeky grin. "One that will do housework and cooking?"

"What? So, I won't have to put up with eating your half-baked pies," Jake teased. Anna made a face but remained silent. Troy sighed inwardly. How he enjoyed watching the loving interplay between these caring humans. He envied them as well, he realized. Giving himself a mental shake, he asked, "Jake, what can you tell us about the folks on the vessel?"

"Oh, about that...you two sure did make a splash!" Jake replied with a chuckle, "The commander had to pull in a lot of markers to keep this whole episode out of the media, I can tell you."

"Many thanks to him for that," Troy replied sincerely. "We really do not want to attract attention to ourselves, to the disaster and damage on the oceans, yes, but not to ourselves."

"Well then," Anna quipped, "you should stop doing these outrageous stunts!"

Jake continued, "Those ships were indeed trafficking drugs, and humans for the North American sex trade, as well as netting and illegally canning certain endangered sea creatures. It's an exceptionally large and corrupt organization. We don't know where it originates or by which country they are sponsored, but thanks to a little tact with media, we are getting some sound leads in that direction. Those people aboard the first ship are singing loudly, babbling about aliens and space crafts and green men chasing them. Oh, and the aircraft that fired on you was US military. Our governments are checking into this. Why were they nearby? Who alerted them and why fire upon you so near to Canadian waters? This could have triggered an international incident, and nearly caused us to abort the whole mission, but thank goodness you tricked your way out of that situation."

"Yes," Anna asked, "how do you get that huge craft to turn 'on-a -dime' as they say."

"It has to do with rotative angles and the forward and rear thrusters," Troy answered with a shrug. "Wayne says Kevin and his family will be here for the Thanksgiving weekend. I plan to speak with him then about allowing the local university to examine our crafts once I have the approval from Central Command on Xernex." This was only partially true since Troy had no idea as to how much longer their mission here on earth would last, nor how much the Intergalactic Council would allow earthlings to know about them being here. So far, they had not encountered any other off-earth travelers here now; best to keep it that way.

***

During the following weeks Brad and Troy made several excursions north along the Canadian Coastline and out to sea beyond the continental shelf, mooring occasionally to let Brad do more in-depth research into the flora and fauna of the area. They made regular reports for Xernex and alerted the Coast Guard of anything that may be of interest to them. Both men were pleased with their work thus far, as were their supervisors. When Troy last reported to Central Command, Syvers suggested that they move on to more southerly waters and check on the huge garbage pools in the ocean around Earth's equator. As well, they were now given permission to contact Raj and Maria.

"The wavelength used to contact Xernex has not been compromised, but Raj has detected a possible infringement on his frequency," Syvers warned, "so we are setting up a new channel for your inter-communication while on you are on Earth. We will let you know as soon as it has been set."

"Okay, it will be great to be in contact with the other two again. How are they faring?" Brad asked.

"As well as you two," came the reply, "though Raj, too, lost a teammate—not during landing, but because of the war they are enmeshed in."

"Oh, I'm sorry to hear that," Troy replied sincerely. "Has Ben, the commander, had any news of my father?"

"Oh yes, he asked me to have you try to contact Ches telepathically again, Troy. We had information about him a while back, and we were told he was slowly limping his way back to Fentanys. Ben hasn't been able to rouse your father and would like you to try. Can you do that, Troy?" Syvers asked.

"Yes, tell Uncle Ben I will do so, and I will get back to you as soon as I do."

"Good, but be very careful, Etrogylus. We do not want to draw unwanted attention to us or to Chestrygus' mission."

"Understood," Troy said solemnly.

That evening, Troy sat out on the deck wearing a warm jacket as the evenings were cooling now in the autumn season. Gazing up at the cloudless star-studded sky, after a brief meditation for protection for himself and his father, he tried to visualize his father. This was difficult since he had not seen the man in many years. Troy remembered the last time he had contacted his father telepathically. It had been while still on the Xernex, before landing on earth. He had a difficult time getting through to his father then as well. Ches did not like others 'getting into his head', but when they had made contact, Troy remembered his father as being friendly but cautious. Would he respond now... could he?

After trying again unsuccessfully, Troy became frustrated and decided to take a walk along the beach. The air was cool with a slight breeze that ruffled his hair and soothed his skin. A lone nightbird could be heard in the bush to his left, while to his right, the water calm and clear with the moon reflecting brightly on the surface of the sea. A soft splash sound caught his attention, and he glanced out to sea to see a pod of whales or dolphins gliding in the water near to shore. Troy moved closer to the water, sat down on a log near the water's edge and watched, intrigued, as the pod-they were dolphins-swam closer. One rose high in the air and whistled, "Quiven?"

Delighted, Troy moved to water's edge, "Kevin's friend you are?"

"Click, click."

"Welcome! Found our new home you have."

The dolphin, Ancion, Troy remembered, chattered happily as he swam even closer. Brad came running down the beach to join them.

"Wow, what a treat that they should arrive just now!" he said breathlessly. "Kevin just contacted to say they would be here for Thanksgiving next weekend and to keep an eye on the dolphins as they have been more active again recently. He is excited to see us again!"

"Great!" Troy replied, then turned to Ancion, "A message for Kevin, you have?"

Ancion just swam in circles then moved closer to chirp loudly.

"In danger your pod is?"

"Click."

Puzzled, Troy glanced at Brad who shrugged helplessly.

"Must help me understand you, Ancion."

Again, the big dolphin moved in agitated circles clicking loudly. Then he stopped in front of Troy and mouthed something that sounded like 'fire' or 'sire.' Troy opened his mind to the dolphin telepathically, now beginning to listen to the chatter with an inner knowing.

"In danger your sire is," Ancion's mind said.

"A message from my father. How can that be?" Troy wondered aloud.

"A message, our family on Ojesta send to Quiven for you."

"Ojesta is where?"

"Far galaxy."

Troy, getting very frustrated now, turned to Brad to explain.

"There may be dolphins on another planet who can communicate with these on Earth. It's possible, you know, if you are to believe some of the Earth myths, like that of Atlantis," Brad suggested.

Troy stared at Brad briefly then turned back to Ancion to speak telepathically again.

"Contact your family on another galaxy you can?"

"Click, click."

"Tell my sire to contact telepathically, you can?"

After more agitated circling, Ancion replied with a "Click, click."

"Thank you. Be here next weekend, Kevin will, Ancion. See him you will?"

"Click, click." The big dolphin leaped high in the air, twisted, and splashed down, then he swam strongly to join his pod further out to sea.

"Wow! Just Wow!" Brad exclaimed. "We have to call Kevin."

"Yes, and alert Ben; I think my father may be in danger somewhere near that place...Ojesta, or some such name Ancion mentioned. I hope Ches can contact me now. Can earth species really contact other planets, I wonder? Humans can't so far, can they?" Troy pondered.

"Well, let's get back and have Cee do some research on that while I call Kevin and you contact Ben."

"All right, good plan," said Troy.

***

The next evening, Troy tried again to contact his father and this time he was successful. Ches wanted Troy to let Ben know that he and the crew were safe for now, but their situation was dire.

"We are in very short supply of potable water, food and fuel, Troy," Ches commented, "our position is just beyond the Ra galaxy where you are, but we don't have the power to get there or to return to Fentanys. Let Ben know. He could send out a forward guard to bring supplies...or better yet, he could tow us to a place where we can do repairs."

"Can you communicate instrumentally at all?" Troy asked.

"Negative."

Troy glanced at Brad who was waiting for information, then decided. "Dad, I'll let Ben know in the morning and let him decide where to go from here. Then I will contact you telepathically again tomorrow evening. Would that work...or maybe get your dolphins to contact the earth pod and let us know the plan?" Troy added cheekily.

With a raw chuckle, his father added, "A dolphin-like animal is the dominant, or prime, species here. This planet is mostly water, but it is very saline, and the land is Earth's deserts. The air is heavy, with less oxygen content than Earth, and the gravity pull is stronger. The dolphins are friendly, but far more primitive than Earth humans technologically. An interesting study this place is, but not sustainable for human life for any length of time, so we need to move on."

"Then we best get you out of there. Be patient, dad; I'm sure Uncle Ben will find some sort of solution. We will communicate tomorrow."

"Affirmative, thank you son."

Troy told Brad all he had learned, and they tossed around a few ideas as to how to aid Ches, but soon decided to let the decision rest with Ben.

"But, how exciting!" Troy exclaimed, "to have discovered a new galaxy and had time and opportunity to study one of its planets first-hand. I really admire my father's work. It must be so gratifying to step into unfamiliar territory like that."

"And a bit scary I would think," Brad commented.

It took several days of communicating back and forth before a viable plan was formulated. Xernex would leave a small satellite in earth's outer orbit to aid the landed parties, then fly at top speed toward the furthest reaches of the Ra galaxy near to Ches' position. From there, depending on how far Triton may have traveled, they would determine the next step. This would mean Troy and the others on Earth would be on their own for months, or possibly years, with Syvers acting as Assistant Commander and Troy himself being the prime coordinator for the landed parties. They would be in constant contact with Maria and Raj, and each would continue to work according to their preplanned agendas, reporting to Troy and Syvers as needed. For the landed parties, this meant a minor change in the original plan, but the timing for their evacuation from Earth would be indefinite. Both Raj and Maria were happy with this plan, and they were excited to share their findings with Troy and Brad. The Commander, Ben, discussed the parties' mission and findings to date with Troy, giving him the new contact frequency and several hints as to how to proceed with both Raj and Maria.

"Raj, having found himself to be embroiled in a local military conflict, has done some interesting studies on the effect of their modern weaponry on not only the population but on the land itself. The pollution of much-needed arable land with chemicals and debris from these weapons is a topic close to his heart, and he will expound on it anytime you care to listen," Ben stated with a chuckle. "Maria has entrenched herself into an ancient African tribe that may have direct connections to our Serian ancestors. This tribe, according to Maria, has lived outside of the influence of the modern world as nomads in a very isolated area. Recently however, a large military base was built nearby, disturbing their ancient way of life. Noise pollution and how it effects these tribes physically and mental is one of her major concerns. And you two have made great strides in evaluating the pollution in the ocean near Canada. I would say you are all accomplishing what was mandated for this mission by the Intergalactic Council, but there is still much to be done."

Troy said, "Thank you, sir, I appreciate your sharing this with me. There is a question I have. Kevin and his coworkers are diligently working with Earth's leaders to rid the oceans of pollution, and he is very anxious to have the knowledge and use of our submersible and launch craft to aid their work. How much of our science and technical knowledge are we allowed to share with the human population, sir?"

Ben thought about this for a moment, then advised Troy to try to maintain anonymity and stick with their back story for now.

When Troy shared his concerns regarding his father's predicament, his uncle responded gravely, "Space travel always involves risks, Troy," Ben reminded him. "But Ches is smart and innovative. We can only do our best and pray it is enough. You too need to be aware, vigilant, and smart. The continued success of this Earth venture now rests on your shoulders, son. I have every confidence you will handle it well."

"Thank you, sir; I shall do my best."

"That is all we can ask. Go with God."

"Godspeed to you as well," Troy replied.

Chapter 16

The highway to the ferry terminal at Horseshoe Bay was congested with traffic despite the high winds and heavy rains. A quick check of the weather channel had assured Kevin that the ferries would be in operation. "Thank goodness you are all good sailors," Kevin told his family as he angled their motorhome into the proper lane to await the ferry for the Sechelt Peninsula. "We could be in for a rocky ride."

Kevin and his family were heading up to Powell River for the weekend, and Nancy and her son Jimmy would be flying in from Comox later that day. Kevin was anxious to meet up with Troy and Brad again as well. Those two, he had heard, were making quite a name for themselves. "I hope the weather clears up for the BBQ tomorrow," Kevin commented.

"Don't worry," Rachael replied with a chuckle, "I'm sure Wayne would BBQ that huge turkey even if it snowed."

"Too true, and it sounds like they are planning on a large crowd. I wonder if Sven will show up."

"I don't know," Rachael replied, "when last I spoke with Nancy it didn't sound like they were anywhere near working through their marital problems. It's hard on her and on little

Jimmy too. I'm worried she will just give up on the counseling and let him have the divorce he seems to want."

"Or they could still try to work it out. Give them a little time. Having agreed to try counselling was a good first step, I'd say," Kevin said as the line to the ferry began to move, and he set the vehicle in motion to follow.

Thanksgiving morning dawned clear and bright, with only a few small whitecaps dotting the waters. It was a glorious Fall morning. Both Troy and Brad enjoyed the trip from Desolation Sound to the marina in Powell River, where they moored their small yacht. They decided to walk up to the Warden home, after stopping at the local grocers to pick up whipping cream for the large pumpkin pie they had purchased earlier at the Natural Food Cooperative on Cortes Island. They had been told pumpkin pie was a traditional dessert for the Thanksgiving meal and Brad figured the women would know how to froth up the cream for topping. As they strolled up the driveway, a young women and small boy spied them and walked to greet them.

"Hi and welcome. You must be Troy and Brad. I'm Nancy, Kevin's sister, and this is my son James. Everyone is around back. Why don't you join them there? I'll just drop this...," she glanced inside the package, "this pie into the kitchen and be right out."

"That would be great. Thanks Nancy," Troy said then crouched to face the young boy who was hanging back behind his mother's skirt, "and who have we here?"

The boy hesitated a few seconds then came forward to stand straight and as tall as he could beside his mother. "Hello, I'm Jimmy," he said, reaching out his hand.

Troy bent closer and shook the boy's hand gently. "Nice to meet you, Jimmy, and this fellow here is my friend, Brad."

Brad gave the boy a friendly wave, "Hi there, Jimmy."

Jimmy nodded, then gazing up at Troy, he stated, "You look like Uncle Kevin. Are you my uncle too?"

"Well, maybe a distant cousin, but you may call me Uncle Troy, if you like."

"OK, Uncle Troy," then turning to Brad, he asked, "you too?"

"Sure, Uncle Brad at your service," he replied with a grin as he bowed to the boy, "you can never have too many uncles, right Jimmy?"

"Yeah, and I get more presents at Christmas and on my birthday!" the boy yelled as he jumped up and down gleefully.

"Jimmy!" Nancy scolded even as the men chuckled.

"Sorry mom, but can I go out to the patio with my uncles?"

"May I," Nancy admonished shaking her head, "but yes, run along. I'll be out shortly."

"Grandpa, I brought more people for dinner," Jimmy yelled as they rounded the side of the house to the back yard.

"I see you did," Wayne said as he walked forward; he ruffled the young lad's hair affectionately then turned to the men. "Welcome Troy, Brad. I see you've met our daughter and grandson. You know the others as well. Come on and sit down. Kevin was just explaining about their new mission, planned for the South China Sea this coming spring."

This caught Troy's attention. He glanced at Brad who sat on a nearby deck chair. "Interesting - do tell us about it," Troy requested.

Kevin laughed and said, "I thought you would be interested. Do you remember last time we spoke about how Fritz had been negotiating with the officials from the Chinese government about the pollution problem there?"

"Yes, I do remember," Troy replied.

"Well, since the reclamation project we launched jointly with the Dutch Consortium has been a viable success, the Chinese are now willing to allow us to explore the underwater pollution problem in the East and South China Seas, and even up the Chang Jiang River. Once we have an evaluation of the scope of the devastation there, the Dutch Consortium will be called in to clean up."

"Of course, clean up isn't the only pressing need. Governments and businesses around the world need to find more sustainable ways to reduce pollution and non-biodegradable waste products," John added.

"That is so true," Brad said, but further conversation halted when Rachael stepped out to announce that dinner was ready.

Diner was a joyful, noisy affair. The food was delicious. Everyone seemed to talk at the same time; Jimmy charmed everyone with his explanation about the origin of the Thanksgiving holiday, "Something to do with pumpkins and turkeys." Now, Troy sat on the patio, sated, enjoying the balmy evening and watching Jimmy chase the family dog around the yard.

He turned to Nancy who lounged beside him and asked, "Goodness, where does that little fellow get all his energy?"

"Jimmy's always been an active child. I can't wait for him to go to playschool, so he can run off some of that healthy vigor with other children. Being an only child, well, sometimes it's hard to keep him entertained." Glancing at Troy, seeing his frown, she quickly added, "Don't get me wrong, Jimmy is a great little guy, full of healthy energy and very inquisitive...a typical four-year-old!"

"Are you and your husband...Sven...planning on having more children?" Troy asked. Then glancing at her stricken look quickly added, "I'm sorry, was that too bold a question to ask?"

"No, that's okay, Troy. Yes, Sven and I had planned on a larger family, but we are having some marital difficulties right now and are seeking counseling. I hope it helps; I don't want to bring a baby into an unhappy situation," Nancy added with a dejected frown.

"I'm sorry to hear of your troubles, Nancy," Troy said sincerely, placing a hand lightly on her arm. "Family is important. You all," he raised his arm and gestured around, "seem to be very close to one another. It's very heart-warming."

"Do you miss your own family when you are away for months on end like you are now?" Nancy inquired.

Troy thought a moment as he again watched Jimmy racing around. "To be honest Nancy, I really don't know what it means to have family like you Wardens do. My mother was a busy, renowned researcher. She died before my tenth birthday. Father is the captain of the Titan and away a lot."

"Oh Troy, that is so sad. I can't imagine life without my son. Were you put into foster care then?"

"Yes, in a way. You see, I was fostered onto Xernex at 10 years of age, and I have lived, studied, and worked aboard ship since then, except for a few forays on land to further my education.

For instance, I spent a year in Europe specifically to learn languages," he prevaricated by way of authenticity. He wondered if he had already said too much about himself. "How long will you and Jimmy be staying in the area?" Troy asked, changing the focus off himself.

"I have to be back to work on Tuesday, so we will probably fly back to Comox on Monday evening."

"Listen, Nancy, we have a working robot on board our launch craft. Do you think Jimmy would enjoy meeting one?"

Nancy's eyes sparkled and she said, "You sure don't know a lot about little boys and their toys, do you? Robotic toys of all kinds are the thing for little boys these days. No more 'Cowboys and Indians' for the new generation! Jimmy, come here; your Uncle Troy has something to show you," she called.

The boy pouted a bit at his mother, but then he shuffled over to stand tall in front of Troy. "Yes?" he said.

"Jimmy, your mother tells me that you like robots. We have a real one on our ship out in Desolation Sound. Would you like to come and meet him?"

"Really?" Jimmy's eyes sparkled in delight.

"Really," Troy affirmed.

"Grampa, Grampa," Jimmy squealed and dashed off to Wayne's side, "Troy gotsa robot, and he said I could see it. Can I? Please?"

Wayne glanced at Troy for confirmation then replied, "Yes son, I think that can be arranged."

"Wow, a robot...a real robot!" Jimmy exclaimed as he twirled around in circles until Troy felt dizzy just watching him.

Brad caught Troy's eye with a questioning look, but Troy just sat back on his chair with a silly grin on his face as he watched Jimmy.

Before long, the visit to Desolation Sound took on a life of its own: John and Kevin couldn't wait to see the launch craft, the teenagers were excited to view the strange submersible everyone had talked about, and the women quickly organized a food hamper for tomorrow's lunch at Desolation Sound. The energy was high, and everyone seemed to be rushing around with purpose.

"Wow," Troy commented to Kevin who had joined him.

"Yeah, they can be a bit overwhelming once they decide to do something. But that's my family!" Kevin said with a shrug and a laugh.

Chapter 17

A squall had passed through the area during the night, so Brad and Cee were out clearing debris from the deck of the yacht and the wharf, while Troy checked and tidied the interior of their launch craft. Though he would again remind everyone present of the need for secrecy, he did not want to leave anything incriminating laying around either.

"Captain," Cee called from his position aboard the yacht, "we have company; there is a small, eh, small human wandering up the wharf!"

"Affirmative," Troy replied with a chuckle, "hold your position. I'll be right out."

"Uncle Troy?" Jimmy called tentatively.

"Right here," Troy answered, hurrying down the wharf to greet the family as they clambered out of their yacht. "I see you all made it. Welcome to our humble abode."

"Yes, welcome," Brad said joining them, "I see you brought more deck chairs. Good. It seems warm enough now to sit out here, do you agree?"

"Cee, you may join us now," Troy called, as Kevin and Brad placed chairs around on the wharf.

"Certainly, sir," was the reply, as the robot wafted deftly down the gangplank to the wharf.

Jimmy just gasped and stared at the robot.

Troy walked over to take Jimmy by the hand and lead him to where Cee stood. "Jimmy, I would like you to meet Cee. Cee, he is my nephew, Jimmy."

"Hello," Jimmy stammered, holding tightly to Troy's hand. The adults stood in silence watching this intriguing exchange.

"Hello," Cee replied, then turned to Troy, "Captain, this little human is one of your people, sir. Amazing! Astounding! A small human being, and it is here with us!"

"Yes Cee, he is. His name is Jimmy, and he is called a child."

Troy turned to the boy and said, "Jimmy, Cee has never met a child before. Do you think you could teach him about being a child?"

The boy nodded.

"Would you like that, Cee?"

"Oh, absolutely, captain, it would be an honor. Come along little, eh, little Jimmy. What should you teach me first?" Cee said, extending a metal appendage for Jimmy to hold. The boy grabbed Cee's metal hand and bounced along with the robot.

"How do you walk like that? How come your arm is warm but metal? Where is your mouth when you talk?" The questions could be heard by the adults even as the two walked away.

Brad could not contain his humor any longer. He gasped and laughed and gasped some more. "Really Troy, you could have warned Cee. I have never seen the guy so, well, so flabbergasted!" He turned to the others saying, "Cee is a working robot; Troy has never programmed him to meet children."

"There were no children on your ship, then," Nancy said sadly.

"Troy was the youngest when he arrived at age ten," Brad agreed. "The rest of us were in our early or late teens when we joined the crew on Xernex. So, there was no need for him to program that factor into Cee's memory bank. Bet this will be a great learning experience for the robot, right captain?"

"Yes, yes," Troy agreed distractedly as he carefully watched Cee and Jimmy meandering down to the beach, "I'll introduce the rest of you when they come back. Why don't we all sit down, and Brad and I will answer all your questions; but first, let me remind you all about the especially important need for confidentiality regarding what you see and hear today. Cee, the launch craft, and the submersible are all experimental prototypes that we are testing out."

"Yes," Wayne agreed, "the work these two are doing is astounding, and they have already shared so much with our local authorities. That has been most helpful, but we do not want to jeopardize their mission by drawing the attention of the wrong people. So, there can be no chatting, texting, talking, and no social media posts about anything you see here. It could be extremely dangerous for the men, and their environmental mission could be aborted. Understand?"

"Of course, and anyway, UBC wants first dibs at that craft if it can be arranged," Kevin added with a chuckle.

Troy just grinned at him. Then he turned to give directions, "Okay ladies, if you don't mind staying out here and keeping an eye on Cee and Jimmy, Brad and I will give the men a tour of the launch craft. I will let Cee guide you through later. You will love his galley! Unfortunately, I must also ask that you all refrain from taking photos or writing notes until I have permission, please."

"Darn," Kevin exclaimed with a playful grin, "I guess my memory will have to suffice."

Cee and Jimmy had come back by the time the men finished the tour.

Cee turned to Troy, "Sir, thank you for this experience. This little eh, child, is an absolute delight. I would that we could see more of him. Jimmy says he would enjoy a 'ice cream float'. May I research and serve up one such, sir?" Cee asked humbly.

"I assent to the research, but you need to request permission from his mother before you give Jimmy anything to eat. She, or his father, would be the one with authority over a junior member of the family, Cee."

"Yes sir, I shall remember," Cee replied. Together they went to join the others on the wharf.

Troy made introductions by extending his hand to each person in turn. "Cee, this lady is Nancy; she is Jimmy's mother, and Rachael here is his aunt. Sara is Jimmy's grandmother, and then there is Keira here, she is his cousin." Troy then went on to introduce the men.

"Hello all," Cee said grandly, "Now, Nancy, may I build a float for Jimmy?"

"Cee, why don't you have the ladies join you in the galley and they can help you design that float?" Brad suggested.

"Ah yes, that would be most gratifying; come along ladies," Cee directed in the manner of an olden day's British dandy. The women giggled and cooed as he showed them, and Jimmy, the way to the launch craft's kitchen.

"You would almost think he is strutting, if one can hover and strut at the same time," Brad said chuckling. "And you have just witnessed Troy's teaching technique. He teaches the robot new things by association, that way his circuitry can assimilate the latest information more quickly."

"I see," John said thoughtfully, "so you give him names and the family ties, and he assimilates and relates to both at the same time. Impressive! Now how do you get him to walk on air - and Jimmy says over water too?"

Troy chuckled then explained, "When we were designing the robots, we realized they would need to be able to traverse rough terrain. Inside, a simple wheel system would have done the job, but outdoors, if he were to be of any assistance, we needed to find a better way for him to move about. So, we decided on using what you would call a 'hovercraft' concept and have him float on a cushion of air, and it works."

"Now, I know you have more questions, but I need to share something with you Kevin...again, very confidential...that will impact on the rest of our mission here. As you know, we are most intrigued by your planned mission to China, and I spoke with our supervisors about it last evening. Syvers wants us to hold off on making a commitment of our time or equipment just yet. You see, my father's ship, Titon, is severely damaged and is lost in the ..."

"Deep Antarctic," Brad inserted, "Xernex is racing to the last known sighting of the ship and has left Troy in charge of the expedition here until further notice. He will also be coordinating with the other two parties in this pollution evaluation mission to ensure things go on as planned."

Troy swallowed and said, "thank you, Brad." He really was feeling emotional, and angry with himself for nearly slipping up. "But Spring is aways away yet so hopefully we will have some resolution by then."

"Yes, I can see your need to stay with the mission in hand, Troy," Kevin said, "but both these crafts, and even Cee, would be a great boon to our research as well. Please remember that when you next speak with your supervisors. That's all we can ask."

"I'll keep that in mind, Kevin."

Kevin nodded then glanced out to sea. "Well, what have we here," he exclaimed delightedly, "Ancion!"

The big dolphin had quietly slipped up near the dock while the men were chatting; now he rose, chirping loudly.

"My goodness!" Rachael cried as she came to stand beside Kevin. "He's grown even more. Hello, big fellow," she said, stretching her hand out to the dolphin. He chirped loudly then bounced up to nudge her hand with his nose.

Smiling broadly, Rachael turned to Kevin and asked, "How old do you think he is now?"

"Pacific White-Sided Dolphins can live to 40 years and beyond, so I'd say he is about that now, and he still leads the pod from what we see."

Rachel nodded, "It's amazing how the dolphins still remember you."

"What," Kevin grinned down at his wife, "are you saying I'm so easily forgotten?"

"No, I'm saying that dolphins have an excellent memory, and look how handsome he still is!" Rachael stated, grinning at Kevin.

"Minx!" he replied as he gave her a small smack on the behind. "Go get our food ready while we men chat with this handsome fellow."

"Yes sir," she replied as she sashayed up the gang plank of their yacht to retrieve the food hamper.

Troy shook his head and laughed at their antics.

"Some folks never grow up," John commented with a grin, while Kevin ignored them to turn and speak with Ancion.

"Troy," Kevin called a few moments later, "Ancion would like to speak with you."

Troy walked over to edge of the wharf, "A message you have, from my sire?"

"Click, Click. Moving they are toward Ra. Slowly. Dire their situation is."

"Say to him. Stay in contact he must. On the way help is. Relay that message, you can?"

"Click, click."

"Dinner is served," Nancy called.

Ancion rose high in the air, chirped loudly, sank down again, then swam over to the pod and away. The men moved to join the women in the launch craft for lunch.

After lunch, the family left in their yacht, and Brad and Troy relaxed. "That was a delightful afternoon!" Brad commented. "And, I think we are quite safe in letting the family view our equipment; but Troy, I'm not sure it was wise to have Jimmy meet Cee."

"It was a risk, I agree, but he was very taken with Cee, and..." he added with a chuckle, "Cee was entranced by him."

"As are you. Or is it the mother who has caught your attention, hmm?" Brad teased.

Troy ignored this and went on to say, "I understand children at that age don't have a very long attention span, so something else will probably catch Jimmy's attention shortly."

"But you did invite them back for a visit, next time they are in the area, didn't you?"

Troy sighed, "Yes, I did. It's so easy to forget who we really are when we're around the Wardens. They are so caring and accepting of us. At times, I almost feel guilty about the deceptions we are forced to perpetrate. Are you ever tempted to share things when you are with Magda?"

"Never! But you have been genetically engineered to be like them, so you may have a deeper connection. I don't know about that part of your training, Troy, or how it would affect you emotionally. My attraction to Magda is purely physical, so safe in that respect, but you may need to take care, understood?"

"Yes, I hear what you are saying. The child intrigues me, I admit, but that may simply be curiosity."

"True; so, I heard you tell Kevin we were heading up north again in a few days?"

"Well actually, that was another deception. Syvers suggested we keep this camp as planned but he would like us to move our launch craft to the southern Atlantic area. How would you like to explore the depths of what is known as the Bermuda Triangle?"

"Now that could be interesting," Brad agreed, and they went on to discuss the logistics of this trip.

Chapter 18

It had taken Troy and Brad longer to organize the next phase of their mission than had been expected. A telepathic discussion with Ches had revealed that he would be needing several elements that were not available elsewhere to repair his ship. These elements, though rare, were found in shale rock on Earth. So, with Cee's help in researching, Troy had found what was needed and purchased the required amount. Now they would need to venture off planet again to rendezvous with Syvers on a small space station in Earth's outer orbit.

"We will leave the rented yacht and submersible here in the boat shed. Load the shale into the cargo bay and we'll be off tomorrow night. I'll ask Jake to check on things here when he is in the area," Brad volunteered.

"I was thinking it may be a better idea to take the sub and return the yacht to the rental agency. We don't know how long we will be away after all. But having Jake keep an eye on this site is a good plan," Troy countered.

"Okay, that would work too. You told Wayne we would try to be back by Easter. When is the Easter season anyway, and what does it signify?"

"I think it's in the later part of March or early April. It's a Christian religious celebration. You will need to ask the family about that. Jimmy would know!" Troy replied with a smile, then added, "We should be able to move out late tomorrow evening and meet up with Syvers to get an idea as to how to proceed. I need to review the information Raj and Maria have sent and touch base with them."

Brad said, "Yes, and I'd like to get the specimens we have been gathering into the lab and organized; do some in-depth analyses if we have the time."

***

Several days later Troy sat with his instructor reviewing Raj's and Maria's transmissions. Syvers sat back in his chair watching Troy intently.

"Both of the others seem to have concluded, as you have, that the earth's refuse problem is indeed that…a problem," the instructor commented.

Troy answered, "Yes, I see that. As well, there are several sectors around the world that are working diligently to help rectify the problem. I see that as a good thing."

"Indeed, it is. And, your earth family are very much in the forefront of this new wave of awareness, and they are motivated to finding solutions. The folks in Raj's sector are too entrenched in their battles for revenge, power, and supremacy to see the bigger picture. Thank the One God that there are those humans who do care! Did you note Maria's findings, Troy?"

"Yes," Troy's eyes sparkled in delight as he leaned forward to speak with Syvers, "that is so interesting! To have found an ancient tribe who are a direct starseed of our home planet. We have studied about previous earth landings by our Serian ancestors, but to have found such a viable link. That is so exciting! And to have done studies on noise pollution...that wasn't something we considered in coming here, was it?"

"No, but her finding merit further studies on that subject, don't you agree?" Syvers queried.

"Yes," Troy agreed thoughtfully, "I wonder if our dolphin friends have noted that problem as well? They are a species who communicate and travel by echolocation. I wonder if they have been affected by noise pollution as well?"

Syvers nodded and said, "Investigate that with them, would you Troy?"

"Certainly sir," Troy agreed.

"I would like you to visit Maria at her site. She has been hinting that she may want to remain on planet Earth permanently. This is, of course, allowed. But it is an undertaking that needs careful attention and consideration. I'd like you and Brad to evaluate the situation and report back. Then I would like the two of you to research the great Pacific garbage patch."

"OK," Troy replied, "but I thought you wanted us in the Atlantic, Bermuda-Triangle region."

"No, Raj and his team have had enough of war for a while. They needed a different environment, so I'm sending them there."

"Brad will be disappointed," Troy said.

Syvers chuckled, "There has been much written about the mysteries of that area, but most, I believe, are caused by natural phenomenon and folklore. Raj is pragmatic enough to discover the truth of it. Has your Earth friend, Kevin, mentioned anything more about their work in the South China area?"

"Yes, they still plan to do research there in the early spring season. I would like to join that expedition if I may. And, Kevin's mentor still wants to study our machinery."

Syvers laughed and said, "No doubt they do! Our technology is far advanced to theirs, but that decision still lies with Intergalactic Council, so make no promises yet, Troy."

"Understood," Troy replied, somewhat crestfallen.

***

Troy spent the next few days on the phone connecting with both Raj and Maria. Both were thrilled to hear from him and sent good wishes for the recovery of the Triton. It was decided that the men would, upon landing back on earth, take a commercial airline to western Africa. Maria would meet them in Bamako, the capital city of Mali, and escort them to her work area. Cee would remain with their launch craft at the base in Desolation Sound. They planned on a two-week trip to western Africa where they would be tourists. As both Brad and Troy had valid passports and had (theoretically) travelled in Africa before, they didn't anticipate any problems.

"However," Syvers pointed out, "Troy, Intelligence has alerted us that your 'adventures' in western Canada may have caught the attention of some undesirables, so we need to make some adjustments to your backstory and paperwork. As well, it may be wise not to use the launch craft for a time, once you have landed again."

"How could that have happened? We have been very careful," Brad questioned.

"We aren't sure at this point," Syvers replied. "The chatter we are hearing may be no more than curiosity on, say the part of the American Armed Forces. They did try to interfere when you helped the Canadian Coast Guard capture those illegals a few weeks ago, or it could be something more sinister. Until we have more intelligence it would be wise to stick with the plan to act as tourists in Africa. Check out not just Bamako, but some of the nearby attractions as well. Maria has been there long enough to know where to send you."

"Yes, that sounds like a wise plan," Troy said.

The men brainstormed a bit, conferred with Raj again, and produced what appeared to be a viable plan. Troy would re-enter Earth's atmosphere, via the portal Raj had used, buzz the area around the North Atlantic garbage patch to collect some aerial photography to send to Raj, then he'd sneak back into camp at Desolation Sound. They would let it be known that their latest foray had been successful, and they planned on a few weeks' vacation in western African. Both men's visas showed they had been there before, and to winter vacation in a warmer climate would not seem at all odd.

"I'd like to spend a few days with Kevin in Vancouver to check out their operation and the planning for the spring venture to China," Troy commented.

"Good plan," Syvers agreed, "and is there someone you trust who could look in on Cee occasionally while you two are away, just as a precaution?"

Brad and Troy thought on this for a moment. Then Brad said, "We could ask Jack, from the Canadian Coast Guard to keep an eye on the place when he is out that way. He has met Cee and has seen our machinery. We believe him to be trustworthy."

"All is good then; good luck and Godspeed men," Syvers said, "We'll continue to keep in touch through on-board communications.

***

Their re-entry through the portal Raj had used went smoothly, but the reconnaissance over the north Atlantic garbage pool not so well. Troy had chosen to fly high as air traffic was heavy in the area, but even so, he had to dodge the occasional aircraft and possibly a fighter plane.

"Raj says not to endanger yourselves getting photographs of the area," Syvers instructed, "he will make do with what information he has now."

"It's near time for the sun to set, and we are above the central vortex of the main pool. I'd like to utilize the sunset at our back to try to gain access to the area below us. There is little to see on the surface, but it appears much debris floats below. Raj may want to have a better idea as to the depth of the debris. A quick plunge into the center where the undersea trough is deep could glean us some valuable information," Troy replied. Then, he reminded

Syvers that Raj's ship, though reliable above and on the surface of the water, wasn't as adept at undersea work as theirs.

"Yes, that's true," Syvers agreed, "okay, make the dive, Troy, but be very careful. And make certain that you are not followed back to your base."

"Of course, sir."

Their ship appeared like a slightly shiny black spot when seen from below, or through a camera lens, but in the direct rays of the multicolored sunset, it reflected the light and became much more diffused and less easily tracked. Troy slowed the ship, so it hovered in the sunset's rays until nearing the ocean surface, then he plunged straight down. Once underwater, he slowed the ship even more.

"Wow, this really is a soupy mess. I'm not surprised most surface vessels circumnavigated it," Brad commented.

"The sea life seems to know to avoid it as well," Troy observed. "This mess will be much harder to clean up than had it all remained intact. I mean, larger objects can be scooped up and hauled away, but how do you remove this?"

"Well, for now let's get some good photos for Raj and get out of here. I don't feel at all comfortable hovering in this garbage stew, Troy. How deep down do you think it goes? At this level, the mass has all but obliterated the sunlight. The damage to the flora and fauna here must be tremendous. Raj will have a lot of work to do here just documenting all this!" Brad exclaimed.

"I agree," Troy replied, "I'll follow this trough northward. Photograph and use the remote arm to get samples of the fluid outside. See that effervescence ahead, could be some noxious gasses from the breakdown of the plastics. We need to let Raj know what is out here so his crew can be prepared."

The men worked in contemplative silence for a time as Troy kept the ship moving down and northward. "I wonder if we will have to deal with the same thing in the North Pacific," Brad mused.

"Quite likely," Troy replied, "we are still not below the mess, but I'm going to follow this oceanic trough further north, try to surface and get us out of here. We have enough data to give Raj a good idea of what he will be dealing with. I'm finding this whole scenario to be unnerving," Troy commented with a self-deprecating chuckle, "but we are in the Bermuda Triangle, after all!"

"Don't remind me," Brad said as he shivered dramatically, "just get us out of here alive!"

A few moments later, after much concentration, Troy commented casually so as not to alarm Brad, "Report our exact longitude and latitude, Cee."

"Certainly, sir."

"Why, what's the problem?" Brad asked nervously.

"A slight problem with navigation at the moment," Troy replied, "the ailerons and outer rotational filaments are sticky it seems. I doubt we can climb out of this unless we find a way to loosen them."

"What do you mean, we can't climb?" Brad barked, then he calmed down some and searched the instrument panels. "Can we move deeper, beneath this massive mess?"

Troy glanced over at Brad then nodded. He asked, "Cee, what is the deepest trench in this area?"

"That would be the Mid Atlantic Trench, sir," Cee informed them after a few moments, "but sir, it lies further out to sea and is quite narrow and dangerous for our ship."

"Show me," Brad demanded. Brad and Cee studied the map for a time then Brad turned to Troy and said, "What's our power capacity at present? If we can manage to get to the trench, then follow it north from here, we may be able to get beyond most of this 'soup' and find a level area to set the launch craft down. We need to be able to go out and look at what is interfering with the navigational devises."

"Okay, that may work," Troy agreed after a moment's thought. "Internal instrumentation appears to be working normally, so it must be some external problem. The outer cameras don't show anything extraordinary, but I'm rapidly losing maneuverability."

It took several attempts before they managed to find a channel into the Mid-Atlantic Trench. Then it was a matter of finding the right channel to move northward.

"Man, this is like traveling through a maze," Brad commented nervously, "but the 'soup' is thinning, and the water seems less turbulent. I'll test water samples for toxic elements before we venture outside."

"Good idea; let's travel a bit further then try to find a level spot on which to anchor," Troy decided.

After docking their craft on a level plateau, they donned their aquatic gear, protecting themselves as best they could, and ventured out into the water, leaving Cee in the ship. A first examination of the exterior of the ship showed nothing out of the ordinary. Then on closer inspection of one of the tiny intake valves, Brad spotted a shiny substance on its surface.

"Troy, check this out," he called.

Troy hurried over and asked, "What is that?"

"Not sure," Brad replied, taking out his quistyr and poking at the shiny substance, "it doesn't appear to be animate-neither flora nor fauna-but it is sticky. This could be the cause of our problem."

Troy used his own quistyr to carefully scrape away the substance, which they realized now, was coating not only the intake valves, but the ailerons, flaps, and filaments as well. "I'm not sure what this substance is, so be careful not to get any on your suit," Troy advised.

They worked quickly and carefully to clean the major external navigational equipment. Brad shared a thought, "Let's keep a sampling of this stuff in a sealed container. The Coast Guard may be able to identify it."

Once back on board, Troy checked out the ship's systems carefully before take-off. Once he was satisfied that they could pilot the ship safely, they took off.

"We will need to do a careful day-time inspection once we get back. I just hope none of that...whatever it is...did any more damage," Brad observed.

"Yes, and let Raj know to be aware of what we discovered. When we do the inspection of the Pacific garbage pools, we will need to start at the outer edges, and not plunge blindly into the middle like we just did."

"What? Our intrepid leader made an error in judgement?" Brad teased.

Troy growled a terse reply even as he maneuvered the controls to speed up the launch craft's progress and watched the instrument panels carefully. Then he turned to Cee and said, "Log our immediate coordinates, and give me an overview of what is just ahead and above us. We are out of here!"

Chapter 19

Kevin sat on his deck on a cool late-October, watching the sunset. Though not as picturesque as the view from their cabin on Savary Island, it was a relaxing scene none the less. Rachael had donned a warm sweater and joined him with a contented sigh. "So, what did Troy have to say when he called earlier?" Rachael asked.

Kevin roused himself to answer, "Oh, he and Brad plan to spend a day or two here in Vancouver before heading to Africa. Their latest mission was a success, so they are taking a little African vacation before starting their next one. They had been in the Caribbean checking out water pollution, and they have a few samples they would like to have analysed. Jake, from the Coast Guard, suggested they bring them here." Kevin glanced over at his wife and said, "I invited them to stay with us while they're in Vancouver."

"That's great! I'd enjoy spending time with those two again. Nancy and Jimmy are flying in on Sunday. Jimmy will be thrilled to see them again."

Kevin chuckled, "Not without Cee he won't, and I can't see them traveling by commercial plane with that robot in tow."

Rachael grinned and said, "No, I guess not." Then she added more seriously, "Honey, have you ever thought that Troy and Brad are a bit, well, unusual?"

"How so?"

"I can see where Troy could very easily be a relative of yours, and they are both well-mannered, nice enough guys, but..."

"But what? What is bothering you about them, Rachael?"

"Oh, I don't know. They are both exceptionally talented men, and Brad is...it seems...just a regular guy, but Troy is...well, different. I mean his background would explain his being intrigued with Jimmy. But, oh, I can't explain it. Female intuition, I guess."

"Honey, I'm sure they are both safe to be around, and as you say, their background is quite different, plus both are highly skilled, near-geniuses from what Fritz and I have observed. It is said that animals and children are both good judges of character, and those two passed the test with Jimmy, our dog, and the dolphins as well, so don't worry about it, ok?"

Rachael sighed then said, "Okay, so how long will they be here?"

"Troy said they fly in around noon on Friday and out early on Monday morning. We will have a lot to show them and discuss in that time. I wish they had decided to come by launch craft or at least brought the submersible, but the decision was to leave Cee at Desolation Sound with their equipment and fly to Africa via commercial airlines."

"That makes sense. This will be a holiday, after all. Where in Africa are they going?"

Kevin replied, "Troy mentioned Mali in west central Africa. I remember that their passports showed that they had been to

South Africa in the past, so this may be a new adventure for them. Anyway, I'm sure they will tell us all about it."

Kevin took time off work on Friday to pick up the men at the airport, then drove them directly to the UBC Marine Science Laboratory.

"Good afternoon, Fritz," Brad called cheerfully as the men entered his office.

There was a mumbled reply from behind the large electron microscope that stood at one side of the room. Then Fritz stood, stepped away from the machinery, moved forward and said, "Welcome, Brad, Troy. Come, let me show you our fine facility."

Brad stepped closer to the microscope. "Nice piece of equipment you have here," he commented. "What are you working on now?" he asked.

"Plankton…but I hear you have a few samples for us to analyze. Come along, we will drop them off at the ecology lab."

Both Troy and Brad were impressed by the sophistication of the equipment and by the expertise here. However, several times Troy found the need to stem Brad's enthusiasm so as not to give away their own superior knowledge. For example, when Brad began expounding on the better use of infra-red band fission to enhance the function of the gas chromatograph used for identification of certain chemical substances in a compound or mixture.

"My goodness young man," one of the professors they had met commented with a wink, "you certainly are knowledgeable. Are you sure you wouldn't want to leave that Xernex Project you are working on and join our fine staff?"

Brad gave himself a mental shake and replied, "Thank you, sir, but no. We've still got a lot to do before finishing that project. However, your facility and staff are impressive."

"Fritz," Kevin reminded the older man as they re-entered his office after the tour, "we are having a barbeque tonight. You are welcome to join us."

"Not moose meat, I hope," Fritz replied with a shudder.

"No, just good old Alberta beef," Kevin said with a chuckle, then he faced Troy and added, "Fritz isn't partial to wild meat."

"True!" the older man agreed. "I'll join you then, thank you."

On the drive home, Kevin asked Brad and Troy if they would like to tour Stanley Park and the Vancouver Aquarium the next day. They both agreed enthusiastically.

"Did you know of Rachael's fascination with astronomy? She would like to take you to the planetarium tomorrow evening to show you some of the wonders of space as seen from planet earth," Kevin announced.

The men were silent for a moment, then Troy cleared his throat and replied, "Tell her we would enjoy that."

Both men sat in stunned silence, trying not to gawk, as they got their first real view of the city. They had become accustomed to Powell River, Troy realized, but this was their first venture into a larger metropolitan area. Vancouver wasn't even the largest of Earth's cities that they had studied and viewed holographically. Reality was far...well...far more.

Brad must have been feeling the same awe, Troy thought, when he commented, "My goodness, Vancouver certainly is vast and beautiful."

"We like it here," Kevin replied. "Our home is on the North Shore, up the mountain, just past Stanley Park. We have all the amenities of city life, plus a grand view of the ocean. There's the park, and the aquarium is to the left," he added as they passed a beautifully treed area, and the road began to curve upward.

***

The BBQ was a resounding success. Brad asked for several of Rachael's recipes to give to Cee for him out try out...after they purchased a portable BBQ of course.

"You've even taught that robot to cook," Keira cried. "Dad, we really need to have one of those around the house. Troy, does Cee vacuum and dust as well?"

"We wouldn't want a 'pet' that took away your chores now, would we?" her father replied in a teasing voice.

Keira pouted a moment then asked to be excused to visit her friend down the street for the evening. The two children quickly helped their mother clear away the dinner dishes then hurried off to be with friends. The adults wandered into the den with an after-dinner coffee.

"Our travel agent arranged for a tour guide for us in Cairo, our first stop in Africa, as we plan to visit the Egyptian pyramids. Then, we take a smaller shuttle to Bamako, the capital of Mali, where we will be meeting up with Maria. She will drive us further inland to where she is working with the Dogon Tribe, studying the effects of civilization and noise pollution on these ancient people," Brad replied to John's queries about their upcoming trip.

"So, this trip isn't just a holiday, then?"

"Not entirely," Troy replied, "we have been in media contact with the other two exploration parties, of course, since landing... uh, on Canadian shores, but it will be good to see first-hand what she is accomplishing there."

"Didn't I read something in National Geographic lately about the Dogon?" Rachael turned to her husband to say. "Yes, aren't they one of the most ancient cultures of peoples alive on Earth today? And, wasn't there some speculation that they may have, in the distant past, been descendants of some space travelers from another galaxy?" she exclaimed excitedly.

"Yes," John added, "carbon-dating, and some antiquated petroglyphs, placed their ancestry as very ancient indeed."

"That is very exciting," Brad agreed. "Maria is studying the effects of noise pollution, primarily from the military base, the airport and the gold mines, on the flora, fauna, and humans in the area. I read that the UBC Marine Sciences Department is studying the same problem as related to the oceans. Am I correct?"

"Yes, that's so," Fritz agreed and began to expound on that topic.

"Would you be able to share some of those findings with Xernex, sir?" Troy asked.

Fritz leaned forward, steepled his hands under his chin and grinned. "Well now young man, perhaps if we could come to some agreement...say, you join us on the South China Sea project with the submersible." He added, "we can share our aquatic noise-pollution data with the Xernex."

Troy smiled and said, "I'll think about it, sir."

After Rachael had showed the men to their sleeping quarters for the night - a snug bedroom with a private bath and two comfortable looking beds - Troy turned to Brad with a troubled expression. “Brad, this is getting increasingly more difficult. These folks are so friendly and accommodating that it’s becoming harder not to slip-up and reveal who we really are. Rachael has some suspicions, I think.”

Brad asked, “Has she said anything to you? Indicated that she doesn’t believe our story?”

“No, not as such, it’s just a feeling I get. Like how she was so excited about the Dogon, for example.”

“I think it’s you who are being suspicious, Troy. But why not check her out telepathically? You can do that.”

“Oh sure!” Troy exclaimed, “If she caught on to that, felt my presence in any way, we’d really be in trouble.”

“Well, relax, we will be away Sunday and they will forget all about us.”

‘But do I want these special earthlings to forget me?’ Troy thought with a stab of sadness and a mental jolt.

***

The next day’s trip to the Vancouver Aquarium and Stanley Park was an amazing adventure. Both men were extremely impressed with the park itself: the size of the ancient trees, the verdant foliage, the way it had all been set up to be people-friendly, with pathways to walk and handy benches to rest on. Then, there was the aquarium with its many differing aquatic species. Though now retired, John proudly showed them around what had been his domain...the Aquatic Veterinary Clinic.

"The sad thing is we are still seeing painful evidence of ocean pollutants like that little otter over there," John exclaimed sadly as he pointed to a cute little fellow who, when you looked at him closely, showed he was missing one eye, "gouged out by a piece of floating metal or a fishhook, we assume. He will survive, but with great difficulty in the wild."

"But Kevin and his crew, and others like them, are making some headway in getting this travesty reversed. Thank the One God for that," Troy stated, not noticing that this comment caught the attention of an elderly woman sitting in a wheeled chair beside him.

"True," John agreed, "but will people smarten up quickly enough?"

'Yes,' Troy thought, 'that is the question we need to find the answer to.'

"Well, this has been great, John, thank you. We are off to the planetarium this evening. Are you joining us?" Troy asked, as they moved out of the area.

That evening's trip to the planetarium was a revelation. Both Troy and Brad were duly impressed by the sophistication of the equipment there. Canada had, it seemed, advanced in outer space observations, and obviously had a great interest in the subject. The telescope itself, though not as powerful as the ones on Xernex, still offered an accurate view of the evening sky...the planets and the galaxies around earth.

"Hey," Brad called to the attendant, "can you zero in on Canis Major? Enlarge that star and the area around it."

"Sure," the guy replied with a chuckle, "folks always like to view the Dog Star up close and personal. Not sure what the fascination is. There are other more distant stars that are larger and more spectacular. But there you have it!"

Troy's heart rate sped up as they watched Sirius A spin closer and closer. 'So, that's how they see our home,' he thought, just catching himself in time before speaking those words aloud.

"I wonder what the Siriuns think of Earth? How do they see it?" he asked aloud instead.

Another chuckle came from the attendant who then pointed their attention to the screen on the far wall. "A spaceman's view of Earth from the Milky Way. And, as you seem to know, Sirius is part of the Milky Way. This is a digital enhancement from the latest Hubble Telescopic images. Here you go," he said with a dramatic flourish.

The camera seemed to zero in on the Milky Way, then panned the red, dull orange and brown terrain of the Dog Star, before turning to race past planets, stars, and the sun, Ra, toward Earth. It was a dizzying sight, and from what Troy saw, amazingly accurate.

"Wow," Rachael exclaimed into the ensuing silence, "that is amazing. Is that how Earth looks from space? Is that what the astronaut's see?"

"What of the coloring on Canis Major? Has anyone ever seen it that way, or is that just supposition?" Brad queried. The attendant just grinned and shrugged.

'But pretty damn accurate,' Troy thought, and he caught the man's eye and spoke, "Thank you, this has been most enlightening."

As Rachael gushed with questions and thanks, Troy felt a tap on his knee. Glancing down he saw a cane halting his path. "You are blocking my view, young man," an older woman in a wheeled chair commented in a haughty voice. Troy knew he wasn't, but he bent down to apologize anyway. Then he realized he had seen her before, but could not place her, or where they may have met.

"I am sorry, Madam," he intoned formally as he moved to the side, "have we met before?"

"I assure you we have not!" she said again in a very haughty voice, but she grabbed his hand briefly, pressing a small piece of paper into it and murmured in what sounded to Troy like Aramaic, "Please contact me as soon as possible, son." Troy gave her brief nod and moved away puzzled but intrigued by the exchange as he surreptitiously pocketed the note.

When they arrive back at Kevin's home later in the evening, Troy received a message from Cee and excused himself from the patio where they had been partaking in a late-night snack. He was told he needed to contact Syvers and did so immediately.

***

"Change of plan," the supervisor said, "Raj has run into some serious difficulty and needs to be evacuated from the area immediately. Troy, is there any way you two can be in Cairo tomorrow, instead of Monday? Maria is on her way to meet with you there. Do not contact Raj directly. He has run into some sort of off-planet hostiles who are involved with the fighting in Earth's Middle East. Raj has had to destroy his launch craft for fear of it falling onto the wrong hands but does have means to get to Cairo, he thinks. Don't contact him. He will meet with you when it is safe to do so."

"Understood," Troy replied quickly. "It's still early evening here, so I'll see about changing our flight plans immediately. Are Raj, or any of his crew, injured?"

"Not to our knowledge, no. What excuse can you come up with for changing your holiday plans at this late date?"

"Brad and I will think of something," Troy said. Then, after a few seconds of silence, he added, "Sir, there was an incident today that may or may not have baring on this." He went on to explain about the strange episode with the lady in the wheelchair.

After a moment, Syvers asked, "What does the note say?"

"Only to meet with her at the airport hotel tomorrow regarding a family matter."

"Troy, see if you can get a flight out tomorrow. Book into that same hotel tonight if you can, but do not, I repeat, do not contact her until I have spoken with Ben about this. This may not be related to the incident with Raj, but it bears looking into before we proceed."

"Agreed. I will see to the arrangements immediately and be in touch," Troy responded.

It didn't take long to contact the travel agent in Powell River and have the flight plan changed. She even got them booked into the hotel for that night with no fuss or bother, and with no questions asked.

Troy called Syvers to inform him of the changes. In return, his supervisor replied that Maria was on her way to Cairo, gave Troy her contact information, and agreed to have her meet the men at the airport there the next day.

Troy returned to the patio to let the family know of the fight plan changes. No explanation was necessary, for as John explained, "With things being as they are in the Middle East now, I'm not surprised at the change of plans. I can drive you over to the airport on my way home, whenever you are ready to go."

Troy and Brad thanked Kevin and Rachael for their hospitality and promised to communicate when they returned to Vancouver after their holiday. "Please tell Jimmy and Nancy we are sorry to have missed them. We will see them on our return," Troy promised.

Later at the hotel, Troy gave Brad the details of what Syvers had told him about Raj and why the change of plans. "Thanks for playing along, my friend," Troy added, "I know you were caught out in the cold with this one."

"Yes, well it all worked out, didn't it…thanks to John's comments."

"Thank the One God for that!" Troy replied then stopped short remembering the last time he had said those exact words at the aquarium earlier that day. He turned and shared that episode with Brad, and Syvers' reaction to it as well.

"That is curious!" Brad agreed. "I can't see how someone here in Canada could be involved in what is occurring in the Middle East. But one never knows the power of other off-Earth beings, or why they might be here now, or why they would interfere in local political struggles." He was thoughtful for a moment then added. "Yes, I do believe I remember a woman in a wheeled chair at the aquarium, Troy. She was to your left and a little behind you, in the area where you and John were talking about the little otter that had lost an eye. I didn't pay much attention, and we all left shortly after. Could she really have been the same person you spoke with at the planetarium? I mean, what are the odds," he said with a shrug.

Chapter 20

Once settled in their comfortable seats in the first-class section of the plane to Cairo, Brad and Troy took time to review that morning's events. Cee had called early, letting Troy know that both Syvers and his Uncle Ben needed to speak with him. Syvers had given Troy explicit instructions regarding Raj's predicament, and that both he and Brad needed to evaluate that situation, as well as Maria's, very carefully. Then the conversation with Ben had been guarded, and ...well ...weird. The good news had been that the Triton had made contact, and Troy's father was well. His Uncle Ben had told Troy they planned to meet up with the Triton within a week, and hopefully ferry it back toward Earth's orbit for repair.

"That's good news about your father, Troy!" Brad was saying, "and I think we can figure out what going on with Maria, and her need to remain here on Earth. Raj? It's like you say, we will find out the facts and take it from there, right? But this deal with Mrs. Grenville is a puzzle. Your uncle knows something about this, but he isn't sharing."

"I know," Troy replied with a troubled expression, "and that is not like Uncle Ben."

Both men were lost in thought for a few moments. "What an old lady whose husband owned a vineyard in Penticton have to do with Raj's situation, I just can't fathom," Brad exclaimed. "And her son being an astrologist at the Vancouver Planetarium? Well, there may be a faint connection there, but they both seemed so genuine to me."

Troy agreed, "You know, when I asked Mrs. Grenville why she had the need to contact us, she said the expression I often use, 'Thank the One God', and the way I said it, reminded her of a place where she used to live before the accident that crippled her and caused the partial amnesia she has suffered with for years."

"That is interesting. That expression is a common one used both on Xernex and on Fentanys. But I'm sure other cultures use it as well," Brad reminded Troy.

"Yes, but that and the fact that I understood the ancient Aramaic patois she spoke, caught her interest," Troy said. "However, we agreed to meet with her and her son again on our return, so let's get some rest now and deal with Raj and Maria first."

"Good plan," Brad agreed and snuggled down into his seat.

***

Their arrival at the Cairo airport late that evening was a shock. When they left, the air temperature in Vancouver had been cool with over-hanging clouds and a drizzle of rain; Cairo, even in late evening, was hot, smoggy, and noisy. The men had packed their quistyrs within their luggage, and they had no problem travelling with them, or with their personal communications devices, in Vancouver. Here, their luggage was thoroughly searched, and the PACD's removed from their ears. Heavily armed guards stood everywhere.

When Troy commented on this to one of the more friendly English-speaking customs officers, the man grinned and said, "Ah, you Canadians are so naïve! But I have good feeling, so I will not shoot you today. You go and enjoy our city."

Troy and Brad grabbed their bags and hurried out to the promenade area where they were to meet with Maria. Once there, they glanced at one another and burst out laughing.

"Now, that was tricky," Brad said, still chuckling. "I wonder how we'd have fared without a Canadian passport?"

"I'm just glad I didn't need to find out!" Troy replied with a grin as he surveyed the area. "Oh my, is that our Maria?"

A tall dark woman, wearing what must have been a traditional dress, walked toward them with an equally tall and similarly clad gentleman. They were a stately and distinguished looking pair.

"Brad, Troy, I'm so glad you came!" Maria exclaimed as she clasped both the men's hands in hers. "Please meet Oliberghan Mogapi, the tribal leader of the Dogon. Oli, these are my fellow, eh, sojourners; the ones we spoke of earlier."

After introductions and greetings were exchanged, Maria led the men to an eating area nearby saying, "Let's grab a drink and decide what you would first like to visit in the morning...the museum...Tahrir Square? We have booked you into a small 'Bed and Breakfast' type of lodging near here for the night."

Both Brad and Troy realized Maria was being cautious and keeping up the appearance of them being mere tourists, so they kept the conversations general, asking questions about the city and area. Troy tried to relax. They could get down to discussing business later.

Greater Cairo, they were told, with a population of over 21 million, was the largest city in Africa and in the Arab world. Its hot desert climate and pollution have become a major contributor the health problems of its citizenry. "The smog, at this time of year, has a lot to do with the naturally occurring temperature inversions, but Cairo has a long and interesting history with many wonderful museums, great architecture, and of course you will want to visit the pyramids," Oli pointed out.

Oli's chauffeur drove them to their lodgings and Maria promised to meet with them the next day. Both Troy and Brad were too tired to chat and slept surprisingly well despite the constant city noise and fetid air.

The Turkish coffee served by their concierge was stronger than they were used to, but the breakfast buns were delicious. In answer to her not-so-discreet queries, Troy assured her they would be touring most of the day but be back in the evening.

"Is there a good eatery nearby? We may want a snack before returning here at night," Brad asked. The women immediately brought menus from several eateries in the area, gushing her praise of this one or that. Brad thanked her, and when Maria came, they left.

"How secure are we here in the car?" Troy asked Maria in a hushed tone.

"The driver is Oli's man," was her reply. Troy cocked up an eyebrow as if to say, "so?"

Maria smiled and said, "You are right to be cautious, Troy. In this part of the world most everyone is suspect. But Oli has his own private group - army if you will - who are fiercely loyal to him and to the Dogon people and their culture. Oli and a select few know who we really are and revere us greatly. He has agreed to help us with Raj's problems as best he can, without endangering his own people, of course. "So, we can speak freely here, but be careful at the lodgings or anywhere else, for there are spies everywhere. Right now, Raj is a hunted man. He has incurred the wrath of the faction into which he infiltrated, as well as that of a group of what he and Syvers believe to be off-Earth beings."

"Why would other aliens involve themselves in this local human skirmish?" Brad asked.

"We won't know until Raj joins us. The Middle East has long been the site of major power struggles, and there are huge reserves of natural gas, petroleum, and minerals there. Raj is to contact me, or to contact Syvers directly, as soon as it is safe. You did know he felt it necessary to destroy the launch craft," said Maria.

"Yes, we were told," Brad said sadly.

The three of them spent the day being tourists. Oli joined them for the evening meal before they returned to their lodgings. He suggested that they may want to rent formal suits if they had not brought any, since he would like them to join him at the Cairo Opera House the following evening.

"That would be a marvelous treat, thank you!" Brad replied enthusiastically for both men.

Though they had seen videos and holographic depictions of theatrical performances, neither man had been to a live opera. The concierge, as was her habit, met them at the door as they returned, asking about their day. "We have been invited to an opera tomorrow night. Our host suggested we find a place to rent formal attire for the evening since we didn't bring along any formal dress clothes. Would you know where we could find these?" Troy asked.

She quickly gave them an address, and instructions of how to take the Cairo Metro to a reputable, she claimed, down-town shop. "Which opera are you seeing?"

"I'm not sure;" Brad replied, "we were told a driver would pick us up and drive us to meet our host at the Cairo Opera House."

"Oh, how fine!" The lady exclaimed, then began to expound upon the wonders of the Cairo Opera, which had, she explained, not one, but seven theaters. It was the most advanced cultural center in all of Africa. It featured Western, Arabian, and native Black culture and music. There is even had a Children's Theater and an outdoor venue. "A friend's granddaughter sang there," she said proudly. "You will enjoy the evening, I am sure."

Troy's PACD alerted him to call Cee, so the men excused themselves and went to their room.

"Can you two get to the pyramids in Giza the day after tomorrow?" Syvers asked abruptly when Troy checked in as in-structed.

"That should not be a problem. Buses make runs several times a day, taking tourists out to the site."

"No! Troy, this needs to be a private journey. You will meet with Raj there then continue to Memphis to join his other crew member. From there, you are to make your way to Mali. Maria should be able to aid you in this. And, be sure to show your Canadian flag and passports prominently. Get some Canadian paraphernalia for Raj and his crew as well. The world apparently likes Canadians!"

"Lucky me!" Troy retorted.

Syvers chuckled, "Report directly to me once you have a plan in place to extract Raj. He hopes to reach the area by the early afternoon. Be at the Great Sphinx of Giza. It is a popular and public place with many tourists. He will be near to the lesser pyramid as seen past the head of the Sphinx. Raj says he may have been followed, so plan for divertive action if necessary. Good luck and Godspeed."

"Yes, sir, thank you, sir."

"Okay! Some action at last. All this touristy stuff is getting boring," Brad exclaimed. Troy scowled at him. "Fine, so what's the plan?" Brad asked with an unrepentant grin.

"You're incorrigible!" Troy replied then clued him in on what Syvers had asked of them.

The opera house was indeed a marvel to behold. It was built with superb architecture, was spacious, ornate, and elegant. Though the musical drama was spoken in a French dialect, Troy could follow the gist of the plot, and the music was delightful. During intermission, Troy overheard many languages and dialects spoken. One conversation caught his interest.

"What's Mogapi doing here?" a woman to his right exclaimed in English.

"Who?" her gentlemen friend asked.

"Oli Mogapi. We haven't seen him around here in a while!"

"So, what's it to you?"

"Just keeping my finger on the pulse of things," she replied with an ugly laugh.

"Stay out of it, old girl. What Oli does is none of your business," the man snapped as they moved away.

Later, while discussing the evening over a late-night drink, Troy repeated the conversation he'd over-heard. Oli shrugged it off. "She was probably either a reporter from one of the newspapers or a minor local political figure," he said with a shrug.

Maria gave him a troubled glance, but she said nothing. "So, what's the plan for tomorrow?" she asked instead.

Troy glanced around, then he quietly outlined what they planned to do the next day.

Maria said, "Good, it's time we moved on and got back to Mali, right Oli?"

He nodded at her then asked Troy how he could help.

"Where do we find a reputable vehicle and driver?" Brad asked.

Oli smiled, "No problem there, let me take care of that. What time tomorrow do you need to be in Giza?"

"By early afternoon."

"Fine. I'll have a car and driver come around to pick you up mid-morning. And, when you get to Memphis, you can either continue by road or fly out to Mali. Let us know what you decide, and transportation will be arranged."

"Thank you," Troy said warmly. "Your help is greatly appreciated."

"You are most welcome. We look forward to your visiting our country, don't we dear," he said with a warm glance in Maria's direction.

"Oh, yes, you guys are going to love what I will share with you," she exclaimed.

Later at their lodgings, Troy and Brad shared their thoughts on the opera with the concierge, who listened with avid interested. Then Brad informed her that they would be leaving in the morning. "Our friend is driving us out to see the pyramid sites, then we will be taking the evening train north toward Alexandria."

"Ah yes, the lady who brought here. Now, who is she, exactly? She never did say," the concierge asked eagerly.

"Just one of the students we met at the university," Troy replied in a dismissive tone. "Madam, could you perhaps see to having our suits returned to the shop tomorrow?" Troy asked. But when she dithered about that, he said, "No, no, on second thought," turning to Brad, "we could drop them off ourselves in the morning on the way out of town and pick up a few souvenirs in that international section you browsed while I was trying on my suit."

Brad's eyes lit up. "Sure, that's a good idea," he replied, knowing Troy was thinking to buy a few Canadian flags, caps and such for Raj and his crew.

Once in their room, Troy contacted Syvers, who said, "Your plan sounds workable and logical. I'm glad Maria's friend was able to help. And remember not to draw attention or use your quistyrs. If these are off-Earth beings, they will quickly recognize them."

***

The next morning the men packed their gear, partook in a brief breakfast, squared up the bill with the concierge, leaving her a fine tip, then strolled out to the front patio to await their ride. It wasn't long before a large four-passenger heavy duty Jeep arrived at the door. A tall black man stepped out, introduced himself as Alef and handed Troy a letter of introduction from Oli. The concierge came out as introductions were being made. Alef said spoke with her briefly. She said goodbye to the men and wished them a happy journey, then she returned into the house.

Once settled in the vehicle, Alef asked if they had any preferences as to where to go first. "I was told to be at your disposal but given no specific instructions other than that you were to be at the pyramids of Giza shortly after lunch. Then we are to drive on to Memphis. The pyramids are just 11 miles from Cairo's center, so it won't take us long to get there."

"Good, then we can drop off the suits we rented last night and have an early lunch before leaving the city," Troy suggested and gave the man the address for the shop.

"So, what was it that you and our landlady discussed before we left, Alef?" Brad asked defensively.

Alef chuckled and said, "You don't know me, so you are right to be suspicious," he said as he leaned back to hand an opened newspaper to Brad. "As you can see by the photo, you two and Maria are now linked to Oliberghan, and the writer called you "inquisitive young Americans" and stated, "reliable sources," so I warned the woman that she had better not have been loose tongued where you two are concerned. She got the message!"

"Thank you for that," Troy said to Alef, then turning to Brad, "Americans indeed! Even more reason to stop at that shop for more Canadian flags and merchandise."

"Not at that shop," Alef interjected, "I'll drop off the suits and take you to another area where touristy stuff is easily found."

"That works; is Oli a political figure in Mali or with the African General Council then?" Troy asked.

"Not on a large scale, no," was the answer, "but he is the Chief of the Dogon peoples and has been very influential regarding enforcing human rights, improving education, and trying to find ways to help alleviate the growing poverty in the nation. He is generally well liked, and we are very proud of him and his accomplishments on our behalf, but he has unscrupulous opponents who enjoy making him look bad in the public eye, so we must be always vigilant."

Chapter 21

The desert was hot and dry, just over 40 degrees Celsius, but the air, though dusty, was much less smoggy than in the city thanks to a slight desert breeze in the early afternoon. They had started by touring some of the lesser pyramids, taking a guided tour inside one before moving on to the area where they hoped to meet Raj. At lunch and on the way out to the desert, Alef had clued them into the political situation in Mali, and Troy had informed Alef of what they were about to do. He in turn had offered a few helpful suggestions. Now they were loitering and waiting, trying not to look conspicuous. The brochure one of the guides had given them stated that the venue closed a 4:00pm. It was now almost 3:00pm, and Troy was getting anxious.

"Let's split up and walk around. We may be able to spot him coming. Switch your PACD to our personal channel so we can communicate more easily, Brad. I'll meander along the shaded side of that lesser pyramid. You two branch further out."

"Yes captain," Brad agreed, and he and Alef moved around the Sphynx to the north.

Troy wandered over to the afore-mentioned pyramid. Crowds were thinning now, so it wasn't as easy to look touristy.

Troy lounged with his back against the cool stones and mopped his brow. He didn't have to pretend to be seeking cool shade because between the increased afternoon temperature, and his own anxiety, he was perspiring. Ahead of him, further along this wall, another person was hunkered down on his haunches with his hat pulled low over his face. As he scanned the waning crowd, Troy saw three men dressed in flowing Arab robes coming his way. The middle one could have been Raj. Troy alerted Brad and cautiously moved forward calling to Raj telepathically, "Raj - over here." The person against the wall straightened as though he had heard. Troy was puzzled by this action as he was sure he had not spoken aloud, so he watched this one closely. When two of the Arabians moved away from the centre one, he hurried forward. Then things seemed to happen all at once and in slow motion.

Raj called to Troy and ran forward. Brad and Alef rushed toward him, and the two Arabs turned and hurried back. Troy was tackled from behind and landed face down in the sand with a heavy body straddling his back, pinning his arms down. Kicking, bucking, and squirming, he tried to free himself. Ahead, he could hear grunts and groans, as Brad, Alef and Raj tussled the two Arabians. Someone called for the security guard.

"Troy?" Brad called, "we have Raj."

"Get him to the Jeep," Troy grunted after spitting the sand from his mouth. He again tried to free himself. A swift, sharp kick to his ribs numbed him briefly, so he stopped fighting.

"Halak, no!" the person above him said sharply, and moved off him. "But search him."

This remark triggered his senses and Troy began to fight again only to be yanked upward by two strong hands. It didn't take them long to search him and find his wallet and the quistyr, which the one man handed to the leader. Troy slumped back down to the sand.

"Ah," she said softly. Troy only just then realized that his attacker was a woman. "So, you are one of us," she exclaimed telepathically in his own language as she examined the quistyr. Troy was stunned by this, immobilized for the moment.

"Who are you?" he asked.

They heard the Giza security patrol arriving.

"Halak, you two, go! Run!" she ordered aloud, and she deftly pocketed the money from his wallet, threw it and his blade onto the sand beside him and said, "I'm sorry; we meant you no harm!" Then she disappeared.

Troy quickly sheathed the quistyr and grabbed his wallet as he straightened. Brushing the sand from his face and clothes, he turned to face the security guards. Brad came running to join Troy.

A small crowd gathered as Troy recounted his experience but didn't mention that the leader was a woman. Oddly, he felt the need to protect her.

"Just another robbery," the bored guard concluded, eyeing Troy carefully. "Canadian tourists are not usually targeted. Just your unlucky day, I guess. You won't be pressing charges, right?"

'No doubt shirking all the paperwork involved,' Troy thought. "No, we are heading north today, so there's not much use in doing so, is there?" he added facetiously.

The guard nodded in acknowledgement and grinned. He said, "Wise man, enjoy your holiday."

Before leaving the area, Alef stopped at one of the restrooms where Raj had stashed his luggage. "You may want to clean up and use the facilities. And Raj, I suggest you change to western clothing. You are Canadian tourists, remember."

Troy cleansed himself as best he could and checked his aching ribs. The skin around the area wasn't broken, neither were the ribs, as far as he could tell, but they throbbed painfully, and he would have severe bruising.

"Our mandate while on this mission was to remain aloof of politics," Raj told them when they were on their way south. "But one of my staff, an Israeli man named Mathias, became enamoured with a woman who was part of one of the many splinter groups involved in the fighting. Through him, she used our mission to further her own agenda and spy on other groups. I fired him and banned him from our facility when I learned of this, but the damage was done. Our cover was broken! I dispersed the locals who had been working with us and had my last remaining crew member, Ted, head south while I came this way to meet with you. In the process I had to destroy our robot and our launch craft."

"What about the data you had collected for the mission regarding the pollution and effects thereof in the desert?" Brad asked.

Raj snorted and laughed harshly. "What data? All I can tell you is that all sides...Arabs, Jews, Christians, Lebanese, Irani and multiple factions within each group...have very sophisticated weaponry that is destroying huge sections of the once arable lands. Farmers and other land workers will be finding live ammunition in their fields and forests for years to come. Children will be maimed by exploding bombs and radioactive material. Why do humans do these horrible things to one another and pollute their habitat in the process?" he shouted angrily, then slumped down into his seat exhausted.

The other men remained quiet as Alef drove steadily southward.

"Raj," Troy knew he had to ask, "you say your cover was broken. Does that mean the 'authorities' know you are an alien, an off- earth being? Have you been in contact with other such beings?"

Raj sat forward staring at Troy with a miserable expression, "I don't know Troy. I can't be sure. Ted and I thought that most folk just didn't believe we were nonpartisan, or they were trying to win our loyalty to their own cause. Mathias' duplicity didn't help. That whole political arena is such a convoluted mess!" he said with a sigh. "But Troy, there were a few suspicious incidents and some intelligence that made me wonder, so I spoke with Central Command, and we agreed to disgard all evidence that could connect us with Xernex or Fentanys."

"Man," Troy said, "I'm sorry your experience here on earth has been so, well, so harsh. Once we get to Mali, you and Ted rest and relax a bit. You deserve some down-time."

"Thank you, Troy," Raj replied, leaned back, and closed his eyes.

Troy pondered it all. Raj's problems-something didn't feel right about what Raj had shared with them. There was the woman in Giza who spoke to him and had obviously been speaking and hearing telepathically in a dialect like that spoken on Fentanys. Then he thought about Oli's concerns, and the political unrest in Mali. And, of course, the reason they were here-Maria's wanting to remain on earth, probably with Oli and the Dogon peoples-kept vying for space in his thoughts. Troy's mind was circling round and round until he stopped himself, took a deep breath and performed a quick meditation. The steady forward motion of the vehicle, and Brad and Alef chatting softly, enhanced the meditative stance until Troy relaxed and emptied his mind of all concerns. After asking the One God for guidance and wisdom to do what was to be done, he dozed briefly then woke refreshed.

"Troy, did Raj mention where in Memphis we are to meet Ted?"

Raj roused himself, yawned and replied, "Near to the Imhotep Museum in the Saqqara Necropolis."

"Good," Alef said, "another active tourist site. What time had you agreed upon for meeting?"

Troy answered, "He will try to hang around until closing time and return in the morning if needs be. It closes at 4:00pm, I believe."

"Well, we are too late for that now, but we are nearing Memphis. Did you keep your PACD's?" Brad asked.

"He has his, but I had to defuse mine because it was stolen shortly after I left the Middle East," replied Raj.

"Defuse?" Alef asked.

Brad chuckled, then he gestured to Troy and said, "Troy programmed them so that should they get into the wrong hands, we can remotely scramble the links, programs, and communications bands, so they are then basically useless."

Alef whistled and said, “Very clever, Troy.”

“Raj, give me your coordinates. I’ll try to contact Ted,” Troy said.

“Okay, but I will need to speak to him. We implemented the voice recognition security system you designed when we became suspicious of our staff.”

“That’s reasonable,” Troy agreed. After studying Raj for a moment, he handed him the PACD. Ted didn’t pick up.

“I try again later,” Raj said, returning the device to Troy.

“What are your plans regarding getting to Mali, Troy?” Alef asked.

“We really didn’t formulate anything. Sev…that is our supervisor, suggested Raj or Maria may be able to help us with that.”

“Well, it is about a four-day trip from Cairo to Bamako by land. Flying out by commercial airline from Borg El Arab Airport would take up to 21 hours and would necessitate a lay-over in Turkey,” Alef informed them.

“Only a few hours with the launch craft,” Troy grumbled under his breathe, “Too bad we can’t use it here.”

Alef heard him and chuckled. “Oh, Maria lamented the same thing. Sure, that would work if you were willing to risk being shot down by a missile and cause an international incident! No, sorry guys, you will just have to figure it out like we poor unenlightened Earthlings have to do.”

Troy sighed and asked, “So, these are our only options?”

“Well, you could rent a small businessman’s jet and co-pilot, and I’ll fly you to Mali.”

“You have a licence to fly internationally?” Raj asked incredulously.

"Yes, but only over Africa or Europe; I'm not qualified to fly trans-oceanic flights and certainly not off-planet ones," he added with a teasing grin.

"Troy, I like this guy!" Brad exclaimed, "you think we could lure him onto Xernex and train him up for our next mission?"

Alef sighed deeply and said, "Ah, thanks, but regretfully, I think my wife and children may not approve of my leaving them."

"Well then, how quickly can you get hold of a small jet?" Troy asked.

"Just one phone call to Oli and its done," Alef replied. "Meanwhile, Raj, would you try to contact Ted again?"

Troy handed the PACD to Raj, and this time Ted answered. He was waiting at a bus stop near the museum.

"We are nearby, now. Tell him you will meet him there in five minutes," Alef instructed.

A short time later, Raj spotted Ted. Ted was in deep conversation with a woman. Alef circled the block once then dropped Raj off near one corner and continued around, parking just beyond the next intersection.

"Thank you," Ted exclaimed, "I am so glad you found me!"

"And just in time, too. That 'lady' was quite determined to spend the night with this here Canadian boy!" Raj said teasingly, putting his arm around Ted's shoulder.

Ted blushed and said, "She just wanted my money."

"That too," Alef agreed, "but you guys must remember how very poor most of the population in Africa is. Oh, there are the very wealthy, and a few middle-class citizens, but most eke out a live as best they can, and for women particularly, there are not a lot of choices. A few political figures, like Oli, are trying to equalize the equation, but it's a slow process."

"Raj handed her some money and told her to go buy food for her family," Ted mumbled.

"That's good! Now, let's find food for us then head back to Cairo."

Back in Cairo several hours later, Alef dropped the others off at a small motel complex near the airport. Then, he went to arrange their transportation to Mali, saying he would meet them at the motel by mid-morning the next day.

"Do you two need anything?" Troy asked Raj and Ted. They both looked too tired to care. "Raj, I'll let Central Command know we have retrieved you two, about our plans for reaching Mali, and see if there is any more intelligence regarding your disappearance from the Middle East. You two just rest."

"That we can do; and, thank you Troy, Brad, for coming for us."

Troy nodded. "I don't think we were followed here but be watchful anyway and rest. We will be right next door," he added.

Syvers was very delighted with the news that Raj and Ted were safe and that they were all heading to Mali the next day. "The Middle East was gearing up for a major conflict, our intelligence reported," Syvers warned. "One of them is in Egypt: a rebellion against the authoritarianism called Arab Springs. It would be best if you leave as soon as possible. And Mali, as you know, is under an uncertain peace agreement right now, so make your assessment and get back to Canada as a soon as you can, Troy."

"Will do, sir."

"Oh! And Troy, Ben says to let you know your father's ship is within two days journey of meeting with Xernex, and Ches is ill but not gravely so. Exhaustion, our medical team surmises."

"That is good news. Thank you for sharing that with me."

"Good work, Troy. Keep us informed."

"Certainly, sir."

Troy turned to share the news with Brad, but the man was fast asleep on one of the bunks. Troy quickly showered and turned in as well. He was asleep in minutes.

***

The trip to Mali was long and tedious. Alef had warned them that the co-pilot and another passenger, who was to be dropped off in Niamey, Niger, were told the men were environmental experts visiting Mali. This way, they could safely stick to the original back story if questions were asked, and they had the documentation to support them as well. They would not reveal their destination, however, saying only that they were to meet with a delegation in Bamako.

"I think we can handle that, right guys?" Troy had agreed. But now, after over 12 hours in flight and being constantly quizzed by Mr. Fayed, Troy was getting tired of it all. The man was not just intuitive and suspicious, he was also condescending and rude to the point of being obnoxious. Brad had tried to ferret out some information about the man, but Mr. Fayed would not even reveal his first name or where he was going or coming from. The only thing they knew was that was that he and the co-pilot were acquainted.

"Fasten your seatbelts. We are approaching the Niamey airport," Alef announced.

'Thank the One God for that,' Troy thought, grinning at Brad. Brad was watching Mr. Fayed carefully and didn't seem to hear the announcement.

"Fasten your seatbelt, buddy," Troy said.

"What? Oh, yes, right captain," Brad stammered, then did so. "Niamey at last. I can't wait to get out of this tin can.

"Are you demeaning our aircraft?" Mr. Fayed turned to shout at Brad. "I suppose Canadian aircraft are better, more luxurious, faster..."

"Hey, hold it right there, mister," Brad shouted back, flinging his hand up in the air. Then more calmly said, "No one is criticizing anyone or anything. It's just been a long flight. I, for one, am not used to sitting this long and could use a bit of exercise."

The co-pilot came charging out of the cockpit with a firearm at the ready. "Is there a problem here, sir?" he asked Mr. Fayed.

The man stared at Brad for a moment then turned to the co-pilot, "Stand down, Eristoff. It's just a misunderstanding. Go back in there and land this plane."

Eristoff look suspiciously from one man to the other, made brief eye contact with Raj, then nodded at Mr. Fayed and stalked back into the cockpit.

'Who are those two?' Troy wondered, 'Alef had better explain once we set down!'

Alef circled the airport once then began his approach, only to rise and circle again before attempting another approach. He finally set the plane down safely after a rough landing.

The co-pilot came forward immediately to escort Mr. Fayed off the plane with no comment or even a goodbye. Brad hurried over to where the man had been seated. He checked in and under the seat and in the crevasse between the seats. Raj rushed forward. "Brad, what are you doing?"

"Back off Raj," Brad hissed, then he placed his finger over his mouth in a "be quiet" gesture as he removed a crude listening device from between the seats where Mr. Fayed had been seated. At a 'go ahead' gesture from Troy, Ted joined Brad in searching the area.

Alef came out of the cockpit, but at Troy's signal, he stood aside waiting. Raj tried to grab the device as Brad handed it to Troy but backed off when Troy glared at him with silent menace.

Then they found it - a small crude explosive device. Ted gestured for everyone to get off the plane then cast a questioning look at Troy. Ted was Raj's navigator on this mission, but he was also a munitions expert Troy remembered, so he gave Ted a nod, and he and the others rushed out of the plane. Once outside, Troy immediately smashed the listening device and turned to Alef. "Who are those two?"

Alef looked genuinely troubled, glancing back at the plane, and he said, "I don't know but I will make sure they don't leave the airport."

Troy nodded then whirled to face Raj, "And you...what do you know of them?"

"Troy, you can't think I would have anything to do with this," he protested loudly. Troy just glared at him until he subsided. "I think Fayed may have been following me since I left Istanbul," he offered. Troy watched him closely then nodded.

"But why, Raj? What have you been doing to warrant such attention? Our mandate on this mission is to observe only, not to draw attention to ourselves. What happened, Raj?"

"Yes, Raj, what did you get yourself involved in?" Brad asked gruffly.

"I think I can give you the answer to that," Ted exclaimed as he hurried down the steps from the plane with the dismantled explosive device in hand. Alef and a security officer stood by watching this exchange with avid interest.

"Inactivated?" the officer asked Ted, who nodded in reply. "Then I'll take that. Alef, secure the airplane, and why don't we all adjourn to my office and straighten this out?" This was not a suggestion, they knew, so the men followed him inside.

Chapter 22

It was not until early afternoon the following day that the men were allowed to continue their journey to Mali. Alef had informed Oli of what had caused the delay, and Troy had told Syvers about it after the officer had taken Troy, Brad, and Alef to an office building near the airport. After a lengthy interrogation, the officer and a local constable concluded that the Canadians were exactly as they purported to be, so they were not jailed. But they were told not to leave the city until further notice. Raj and Ted were released the following morning and the men were told that they could continue their journey. The co-pilot and Mr. Fayed remained in jail pending further investigation.

"This leaves us without a co-pilot," Alef complained. "I doubt I can find a replacement on such short notice."

"May I have a look at the instrument panel, Alef?" Raj asked. "It was years ago, but I have piloted carbon-fuel-powered machines in the past."

"Sure, let's see what you remember!" Alef replied eagerly. "If you think you can manage to assist, we can leave soon."

Alef came back to the terminal later. "Okay guys, all aboard! Raj and I will do a pre-flight inspection, then we are on our way."

"Well, about time!" Brad stated, grinning.

Once they had attained their flight path, Troy joined the men in the cockpit.

"So, how's it going?" he asked Raj.

Raj grinned and said, "Well, it certainly isn't the launch craft, but a pretty sophisticated little machine for its day."

'He looks more relaxed than he has since we had met up,' Troy thought, 'like Father, Raj may just be exhausted.' After chatting a bit longer, Troy returned to his seat. "Ted, what can you tell us about what happened?" he asked.

"Obviously, the commander hasn't told you," He replied with a sigh. "As well as being the navigator on Raj's ship, I am a munitions expert - one of the Xernex Security Detail."

"Man, you've been spying on us!" Brad exclaimed.

"Yeah," Ted grinned, "and that little lady you have been seeing isn't cheating on you, in case you wondered." Brad laughed, and Ted continued, "I'd been training with all of you for the Earth mission. The Commander-in-Chief realized Raj had been disgruntled when you were given command of a ship, Troy, so I was placed with his crew to keep tab on things. It's what I am trained for."

"You look far too young to be a spy," Troy commented.

"And you are very young to hold command," Ted countered with smug grin, "I'm several years older than you, Troy. My youthful appearance and demeaner are an asset in my work."

Troy chuckled and said, "Okay, I'll give you that one! But tell us, what was Raj doing to get himself in this mess?"

"I am not sure how it started. We were working in an active war zone, don't forget. Hostilities were not always overt, but there was constant fermenting unrest. Raj abhorred what the humans were doing to one another and to their environment. Unbeknownst to the rest of our group, he must have become involved with, or sympathetic towards, one of the splinter groups in the area."

"I'd never have thought that of Raj. He always seemed so stalwart, so by-the-book," Brad commented.

"We witnessed some very disturbing sights, believe me. I know that the ones involving exploitation of children really bothered him. What I surmise is that when Mathias's duplicity became known, Raj realized he needed to extract himself from whatever it was he was involved in. I had suspicions before that but could not prove anything."

"But your back-story wasn't compromised, as far as you know?" Brad asked.

"I don't think it was. Raj told Syvers he had destroyed the ship, and that his PACD was stolen. I can't find evidence either way. He has been very secretive and clever."

"What of the intelligence of other, possibly hostile, off-earth beings?" Troy asked.

"There are rumours to that effect, yes, but again nothing definitive. It's very frustrating. Oh, and to make things worse, our robot has disappeared!"

"Have you defused it?" Troy asked.

"When Raj reported it missing, I too tried to contact the robot. When it didn't reply after several attempts, I remotely defused it, yes."

"This is all very curious," Troy pondered. "Hopefully, Raj will shed some light on it all. I wonder where Mr. Fayed fits into this equation, if he does? Alef may have some ideas about that."

The three men remained in silent contemplation as the plane winged its way toward Bamako. Upon arrival at the airport, Alef introduced the men to a tall stately black lady with a mass of kinky graying hair, sparkling chocolate brown eyes and a broad smile. "Sister Angelina, these are the Canadians Oli will have told you about. Troy, Brad, and Ted, I'll leave you to the Sister's care. Raj, grab your luggage and came with me. Sister, will Esme be well enough to travel back with us?"

"Yes, she is doing well, thank you Alef."

He nodded and said, "Okay, let's all meet at the plane at 11:00am tomorrow. Would that suit you?" he asked, glancing at Troy. Troy nodded and Raj left with Alef.

"Well, come along then lads," Sister Angelina called as she hustled them toward the exit and an antiquated jeep that sat parked in a no-parking zone. She gestured for them to stow their luggage in the back then climbed into the vehicle. The men were too stunned to do otherwise. Once she herself was settled behind the wheel, she glanced at Brad sitting beside her then turned to Troy and Ted in the back seat. "All set?" she asked. "Good, then we're off."

Sister Angelina gunned the motor, blasted her way into the line of traffic amid the blare of horns, angry shouts and shaking fists. She grinned and muttered something that sounded like, "grey female power!" as they exited the airport area and headed into town.

Brad said, bent over laughing, "A grey-haired feminist nun!"

"You'd better believe it, sonny!" she declared. A short time later she whipped the vehicle down the curved driveway of the Residence Les Fleurette and came to a shuddering stop at the front door.

A man hurried out hauling a luggage cart. "Ah, Sister, you have arrived! Come, come," he gestured to the men, and he loaded their luggage onto the cart. "I will show you to your suite. Do you stay, Sister, or return to the hospital?"

"I'll be back for the evening meal," she remarked to Troy, then she climbed back in the jeep and shot off amid the squeal of brakes and honking horns.

"Does Sister Angelina always drive like that?" Ted asked astounded.

"Oh yes, our Sister, she is a good driver, yes?" came the proud reply.

Later at dinner Sister Angelina told them about herself. "I'm not really a nun per se," she confessed. "We are a group of women from many walks of life and various religions who are dedicated to raising the standards for women in our world. Oliberghan Mogapi, his father before him, and the Dogon tribal leaders have been most helpful in getting this project underway."

"So, calling you 'Sister' is a title?" Ted asked.

"It's an honorific title, yes," she replied.

"At school we call her Mother Angelina because she is the best mother we know," Esme said shyly. The girl had been transported to the Bamako Children's Hospital for major surgery and would be traveling back to the Dogon territory with them.

"Thank you my dear," Angelina said, giving the girl a quick hug.

"So, you run a school?" Troy asked.

"Yes, our group runs a school for girls. We also have a clinic with several doctors on staff, and we offer different classes to adults for everything from personal hygiene and birth control techniques to money management. We encourage our people to maximize their own talents."

"Wow, that's an accomplishment!" Brad exclaimed. "How long has your group been in existence, and how, of I may ask, are you financed?"

"Our organization, Ladies First, was founded in 1978. We try to be as self-sufficient as we can, and we are associated with several international aid organizations, like CUSO. We manage. The One God always provides," said Sister Angelina.

"Interesting!" Troy exclaimed. "I read that in Mali the population is divided almost equally in their faith practices between Christian and Muslim teachings. In the rest of the world, these two religions are in constant conflict with one another, but here in Mali, I understand, you work and dwell together in peace. Why is that?"

Angelina's eyes sparked delightedly as she replied, "Ah, yes, I'm so glad you realized that fact. While we may practice our religious faith in diverse ways, the Dogon, particularly, still adhere to their cultural roots. Whatever our religious rituals, we still all worship, revere and honor the One God. We have learned to respect other people's ways of worshiping, and we try to work together to fight the ignorance and poverty, rather than fighting with one another. It is as simple as that."

"Wow," Ted said in awe, "that is profound."

"Come, Esme," Angelina said, "we need to get you to bed. We will meet you boys for breakfast, yes?"

"Sounds good," replied Brad as the others nodded.

"I'll leave the Jeep here, so be prepared to board the airport shuttle-bus by 9:00am."

"Will do," Troy agreed.

"What, she's not driving? What a relief!" Brad murmured under his breathe.

"I heard that young man," Angelina said severely, then turned and chuckled softly as she and Esme left the dining room.

"What an amazing woman!" Troy exclaimed, and the others agreed.

***

The flight from Bamako north to Bandiagara, the area near one of the Dogon communes, took about an hour and a half. Several vehicles were waiting there to take them to Oli's compound. The air was hot and dry but not smoggy like Cairo. A ridge of low mountains or escarpments was visible in the distance and a wide river flowed sluggishly beside the road upon which they traveled. Troy had read that the Niger river and its tributaries was the main source of water in Mali and that it flowed in the southern part of the country, while the north was mostly desert-like. Only just over 5.5% of Mali's land was arable, but the expanding irrigation system, first installed some years ago, was opening more land to farming and reforestation. Though far different from Canada's west coast, Mali too had its charms, Troy decided.

The compound lay on the plateau between the river and the Dogon Escarpment. It was a commune with a small village and market at the center. The Dogon Communes were designated World Heritage Sights, and tourism had become one of their more lucrative industries. Most of the buildings were constructed of mud wattle, river gravel and wood. Though the wood, they were told, was a scarce commodity now, so different from the lush Canadian forests. The commune was comprised of one long two-storied building surrounded by numerous huts and garden plots.

Maria rushed out to greet them wearing a colorful flowing caftan-like dress and a fancy turban headgear. "Oh, I am so glad you are all here safely. Esme, are you well? Come in, come in out of the heat." Inside, the building was cool and surprisingly modern. A servant hurried to take their luggage. "Ramsun will show you to your rooms, so you can freshen up then join us in the lounge," Maria instructed the men, pointing to a tall man in a distinctive deep purple tunic. "Angelina, Esme, come with me."

The building, they now realized, was in a U-shape with two wings extending to the back. The upper level was designed as a small hotel. Each of the men was assigned a separate room. "Bathrooms are in the centre, and there is a small lunchroom behind the meeting area. Please feel free to partake. Maria would like to meet in half an hour. The lounge is down the stairs and to the left. Enjoy your stay with us," Ramsun said warmly.

Troy's room was small but adequate with a single bed, dresser, wardrobe and a small desk and chair. The one window faced the river and the plateau beyond, with low hills in the far hazy distance. Heat waves shimmered over the landscape, but inside, the building was pleasantly cool. Troy, like the others, made use of one of the four bathrooms to freshen up before going downstairs to the lounge. Maria, Alef, and Angelina were waiting, and Oli joined the group shortly after.

"How long had you planned to stay before returning to Canada?" Oli asked.

"Just a few days, I'm afraid," Troy replied. "Our supervisors have suggested we leave the area soon because of the growing unrest in northern Africa now."

Oli nodded thoughtfully, then they discussed an agenda for the time that the men would be spending in the compound, for, as Maria had pointed out, there was much they would want to see. Troy, Brad and even Raj were excited to hear about the link between these people and their own homeland, and they were anxious to learn as much as they could.

***

After a delicious dinner of home-grown produce, they again retired to the lounge area. "Raj, would you like to share with us about what had happened to you and your crew since landing on earth?" Troy asked, before another discussion could be started.

Raj glanced around at the others, looking decidedly nervous and sad, Troy thought. Troy silently said a quick prayer asking the One God for wisdom, to deal with whatever arose now, then he leaned forward encouragingly toward Raj. Raj glanced at Alef, who also nodded his encouragement.

"We made a safe landing on an unpopulated desert plain near Kandahar, not far from the Afghani border," he began, "and we soon found a cave in the nearby mountain in which to hide our launch craft. We quickly contacted the few desert peoples who, though suspicious, seemed to tolerate our presence there at first," he said with a long sigh. "We employed a few locals to help set up a desert camp and reconnoiter the area. It didn't take us long to realize that we had stumbled into a local war zone. When one of our crew was killed during a scrimmage, we decided to leave the robot with the launch craft, camouflaged the cave we were using as best we could and headed into the largest local town to find out how best to proceed with our mission.

"Did you contact Syvers at this point, Raj?" Brad asked.

"Yes, I followed procedure, telling him of the death of our crew member and our plan. He agreed to the plan but advised extreme caution."

"Why not have you move to a safer desert location?" Maria asked.

Raj just shrugged and continued with his narrative. "Our back story and credentials helped to pave our way to meeting with several influential local political figures. One such man, El Sayed, was a more forward-thinking man who wanted a better future for his country, so he was helpful in suggesting areas where we may be of assistance to his country, as well as gathering information about pollution. One of his favorite topics was that of how to get the desert and near-desert areas to be more arable and productive. He was very proud to drive us out to an area near the city where they had formed a small man-made desert oasis. El Sayed then offered us his protection to study that area of the desert if we lent my botanical expertise to the local farms. It was a fair exchange we felt, so after a chat with Central Command, we decided to take him up on the offer."

"Yes, that agreement worked out well for both sides," Ted agreed, "until Mathias and his girlfriend's duplicity got us all in trouble, right Raj?"

"Yes, but there is more," Raj went on to say. "Firstly, the Afghani are very suspicious people who do not forgive slights against them easily, with good reason, considering their history of being exploited repeatedly. And secondly," Raj continued with a heavy sigh, "Troy, I broke protocol."

"How so, Raj?" Troy asked softly.

"I utilized our launch craft for personal use. Oh, Ted wasn't aware, as I always made sure he was elsewhere engaged. But he was suspicious nonetheless, right Ted?"

"Explain," Troy said, again softly.

"While exploring the desert area not far from our camp, my assistant, Jemal, and I came across a heavily guarded encampment," Raj said. "Suddenly, Jemal screamed at me, saying, 'Oh no, oh no; go, go! Drive away fast!'. So, I raced around behind a high dune, stopped the jeep, and demanded to know what it was that frightened him so. He took a deep breath and motioned me to keep driving, so I continued at a more sedate pace so as not to draw attention to us. Eventually, he told his story. It had been during the time of Al Qaeda. At the tender age of 6 years, Jemal and several of his friends were kidnapped and taken to that same encampment to be trained as fighters. He didn't explain much, only that it was grueling, painful, and desperate for him until his father and uncle rescued him from the place. He had thought the encampment was abandoned now. Even though he was still anxious, we all agreed to return at night to see what was really going on there. We discovered that the camp was being used again. This time, young girls were being exploited as well. It was abhorrent to me, Troy. I had to try to stop it! I knew that doing so was contrary to our mission mandate, but I proceeded nonetheless."

"So how did you stop that horrible situation?" Troy asked in a hushed tone.

"We found a kindly group of Catholic Sisters who agreed to hide these children until their parents or guardians could be contacted. Then Jemal and a small army stormed the compound, and I grabbed the children and ferried them to the nuns."

"Ah, come on Raj," Ted chided, "there was more to it than that."

Raj grinned and explained, "Well, seeing the launch craft coming at them with all its lights blazing did a great job! The guards were stunned frozen as I landed the craft within the compound. The children had been told they were going for a midnight airplane ride, but not to say anything. They filed into the launch craft like disciplined little soldiers should, and we were gone in minutes! That did however give rise to the rumors of off-Earth beings having arrived. Desert people are superstitious and suspicious folks."

It was Brad who broke the silence after Raj's recital with a roar of laughter. "Raj, you old sneak. Who would have thought!" Then the others joined in.

After the laughter calmed down, Troy asked, "But why scuttle the craft?"

"I think I can answer that," Ted stated. "Shortly after Mathias' fiasco, a certain group was planning to reopen that training camp for the same purpose, right Raj?"

He nodded resignedly.

"The rumors of other off-Earth beings having been seen in the area, as well as Mathias' defection, convinced Syvers to let you destroy it. But he didn't tell you how to do that. So, you flew it to the compound, harassed the guards until they all left, and set it down in the center of the courtyard after programing it to self-destruct. Did you donate your robot to the Sisters for the children?"

"Yes, after defusing and reprogramming it," Raj said.

Silence ensued for several minutes; then Maria suggested that they should all retire to their individual sleeping areas and partake of a calming night-time herbal tea before bed. "We all need to give ourselves some time to come to terms with the reality of our situation," she advised.

Chapter 23

After Raj's disclosure the night before, Troy found it difficult to get to sleep, so he dressed again and wandered outside to the courtyard area. Maria was awake as well, sitting on a bench in the gazebo-like structure in the garden. She motioned Troy to join her there.

"Are you unable to sleep? May I get you anything, Troy? A drink, a small snack?"

"No thank you, I just need to think things through."

"Yes, that was some revelation Raj shared. I would not have guessed that behavior of him, but we all have our weak points and our strengths. Sometimes what others perceive as a weak point is really our strongest asset."

"How very true Maria," Troy agreed. They sat in companionable silence for a time, both lost in their own thoughts.

"And what of you, Maria," Troy asked, "What is your story?"

She turned to him with a huge smile and said, "My weak point is Oli and his life path; but I do not see that as a weakness. Love never makes you weaker, only ever stronger. Oliberghan Mogapi has a great destiny here in his country, and I believe I can help him shape it for the good without interfering with the natural process of things here. Others of our world have done this before, as I will show you later today. It is so exciting to be here in Dogon country at this time in its history, Troy. As well," she added coyly, "I love that man, and he loves me. I want to bring up our child here in Africa with her ancestors - his and mine."

"You are expecting a child?" Troy asked astounded.

"Yes, isn't that exciting! A truly Dogon child - part human from Earth and part Siriun from Fentanys - just like our ancestors before us."

"Wow! Congratulations, Maria, that is wonderful news," Troy said aloud. 'But that makes things even more complicated,' he thought. 'More complications we do not need!' "Maria, has Alef said anything about Fayed and the co-pilot?" he asked aloud.

"No, he knows no more than we do, and if Raj does, he is not speaking of it. Poor Troy, we have all put you, as our leader, in an unenviable position," she said as she placed a sympathetic hand on his arm. "Try not to stress about it and just relax while you are here. Everything will work out as it must. Thanks be to the One God."

"Yes, I know you're right; I think I will be able to sleep now. Thank you, Maria, and good night."

***

"Good morning, everyone," Troy said after they had all gathered for breakfast. "Before we begin our day, I would like to share with you what Syvers and I have discussed." Glancing at them all, he continued, "Some very revealing news has become known regarding those on our mission. As your Leader now, it is my duty to try to resolve some of these issues. Maria, is your launch craft still workable...that is, can you contact Xernex directly from it."

"Yes, it is, and we can."

"Good, then what I ask is that you and Raj present your case directly to the Commander-in-Chief during a conference call that Syvers and I will set up for tomorrow evening. Uncle Ben and Xernex are out of Earth's orbit right now, but they should be within the Ra galaxy, and accessible by then. I spoke with him telepathically, and he is anxious to hear from both of you. The rest of our crew will no doubt be questioned as well, but I would like to leave it to Raj and to Maria as to how much or how little they feel the need to share with Central Command. And I would like all of us to honor their stance," he added, glancing around. "Is that clear?"

"Yes, and thank you, Troy, you are being more than fair in this," Raj agreed quietly. The others nodded in agreement.

"Okay, then let us finish our breakfast and see what else Maria has to show us."

The group of seven (Raj, Ted, Brad, and Troy, along with Maria, Oli and Ramsun) climbed into an old school bus and headed out across the plateau. Ramsun, Troy now realized when seeing him out of the house-boy uniform, was the second of Maria's original crew. The other crew member, like Ellen, died during the landing.

The land was primarily flat and semi-desert. They passed the ruins of several ancient buildings and sacred sites dating back to pre-Paleolithic times. "The Dogon are one of most ancient of civilizations on earth," Oli told them, and he said that this area was a designated World Heritage site. "We are proud of our heritage, and we have preserved the ancient language and ways of worship, of honoring nature and all life," Oli said. Then he went on to proudly show them the irrigation system they had installed, and the crops that were now starting to grow.

"We have begun a reforestation program," Maria added. "And you may have noticed the raised gardens around our home. Our aim is to be as self-sufficient as we can."

"Our Maria has ordered special mulberry bushes and silkworm larvae from Japan to see if they can adapt to our climate," Ramsun added teasingly. "If so, our women can then weave their own yarn and fashion their own clothing."

The temperature had risen sharply during the morning so that by noon everyone was tired, hungry, hot, and ready for a siesta. All but Raj, who seem accustomed to this level of heat, and was chatting enthusiastically with Oli and Ramsun about irrigation, land usage, and plant species that could be grown or adapted to this climate. Watching them, Troy got an idea.

"Raj," he called, "if the Commander gave you permission, would you consider continuing with your Earth mission in this area? The terrain here is like where you were originally working, isn't it?"

"Oh, Troy, what a wonderful solution!" Maria exclaimed enthusiastically. "Raj could continue with his mission, and we could take advantage of his botanical expertise. What do you say Raj?"

"I would certainly think about it, but yes, such a plan could be the answer for both of us."

'Good, I'll speak about this with Uncle Ben.' Troy thought. 'Now about Maria? Oh yes, and her crew?'

During lunch, Troy brought forward the subject of Maria's desire to remain on planet Earth. Both she and Oli were adamant that this should be allowed. With Brad playing devil's advocate, the discussion became quite heated at times, but humorous too.

Troy turned to Ramsun and said, "Would you want to remain as well?" he asked quietly.

"No," Ramsun shook his head, "I am getting older, Troy, and Fentanys is my home. I would like to retire there."

Troy nodded. "I am sure that can be arranged. Where is your robot?"

"We left it on the launch craft," Ramsun replied.

Dressed in loose clothing, sturdy shoes and wearing hats, the group, as well as Angelina and Alef, boarded the bus amid the mid-afternoon heat.

"We are headed toward one of the largest Dogon compounds or villages and one of the oldest Dogon shrines. It is still in use today. All of these places are part of the World Heritage Site," Oli informed them. "Above the village are the ancient cliff dwellings of our people."

"We ask you to be respectful as we tour the village. The people who live there are ordinary working folks, who sometimes find it a burden to live in museum, as it were," Alef commented.

The architecture fascinated Troy and reminded him of something, triggering a memory he could not bring to the fore. The dried sandstone brick and carved rock, the two-story rectangular buildings, often covered with conical straw roofs, were all somehow familiar. Mali's terrain certainly mimicked the rural areas of Fentanys, though the architecture was not as he remembered. A glance at Brad told him that he too was feeling a familiarity. They would have to chat about this later, Troy decided. The temple was a tall, flat-faced stone and mud building, with numerous rectangular openings symmetrically carved out for windows on two levels. It was topped with nine conical spires extending from the roof. The inside was cool and well-lit with natural lighting. Ornate carvings graced the walls. It was more spacious than it appeared from the outside.

Upon being introduced to the group, the priest acknowledged the party with a bow. "We are so pleased you have come to be amongst us again, dear Siriuns. Come, I shall show you how we remember and honor our ancestors." Then he led them out and around the shrine to a partially hidden stairway set in stone. From the outside, the cave dwellings appeared to have large or small rectangular doorways set in the face of the escarpment; the inside was a warren of hallways and rooms. Light shone from 'doorways' seen from below, which were angled, Troy realized, to precisely catch the sun's rays no matter where it sat in the sky. 'Ingenious!' Troy thought.

The Priest then led them into a large chamber where every wall was a mural, a pictorial depiction of what must have been their life at the time. Some pictographs were etched into the stone wall, others were painted in vivid colors, some were friezes or figures of humans and animals that were, somehow, adhered to the walls. Below, against the base of the wall, sat layers of carved squarish stones on which were painted or etched various figures, pictures, drawings, and glyphs. One larger one showed what could only be described as our galaxy, another detailed the Milky Way.

"Is that...is that what I think it is?" Troy muttered in awe.

"Ah, yes, you recognize the solar system, the Milky Way?" the priest intoned with a smile.

"But how did the ancient humans know?" Brad asked.

"We were shown," the priest said sagely, "by your people who visited us millenniums ago. See here," he went on to say as he picked up another stone pictograph, "this one shows the Sirius A star, you call it the dog star, or Dogon Star. Look closely and you will see another smaller but dense and heavy star circling. It was only after the invention of the Hubble Telescope, that in 1970 astronomers found this star and called it Sirius B. We have known of it all along, for that is where our ancestors came from: Sirius B, Canis Minor, Po, or whatever it is named. It is part of your homeland and the source of our ancestry."

"Wow!" Raj and Brad exclaimed together.

'Yes, this is amazing! What a wonderful opportunity to learn and know,' Troy thought as they continued with the tour before going back to Maria's for supper.

"Tomorrow, you just relax and do whatever you choose. We are going to visit Angelina's school in the afternoon. You are all welcome to join us," Maria announced after supper, before they retired for an early night.

The next morning, Troy checked in with Syvers to see that all was ready for the conference call in the evening which they would, they agreed, set for 8:00pm. Then he spoke with Cee briefly.

"Brad, I called Cee this morning," Troy shared later. "The guy misses us, I think."

"Yes, as much as an automaton can," Brad chuckled.

"No, really, remember last time we left him alone for a time? He was 'besieged by a great beast.' Well, it has happened again - this time by a pair of bears that are lounging in the sunlight on the wharf. Oh, and he has discovered snow- 'glistening, white, ornately designed particles of frozen rain.'

"Cee does have a way with words!" Brad said, still chuckling, "but all is well there?"

"Yes, but we should plan to return to Canada soon." Brad nodded in agreement.

***

The school lay on the open plain near to Oli's compound. It was a collection of several mud, wattle, and stone buildings, that in the afternoon heat, seemed to shimmer and blend into the surrounding terrain. Angelina greeted the party warmly and ushered them into the cooler interior, explaining that this compound included more than just the Lady's First School; it had grown to become a combined trades school and college as well.

"Through CUSO, UNESCO and other aid organizations, we have been able to find qualified teachers and the funds to continue running the school," she explained.

While touring the classroom areas, they suddenly heard a young voice call, "Uncle Alef, Uncle Alef." Alef crouched down with his arms extended as a young girl raced down the hall to be caught up in his arms. “Uncle Alef, did you fly safe?” she asked.

He nodded and turned to Angelina, “And has our girl been good, studied well?” Angelina pretended to consider this for a moment, then she smiled and nodded. Alef placed the girl back on the floor, reached into his pocket, then handed her a big bag of hard candy. “Mind, you have to share with your friends,” he admonished.

She nodded solemnly then turned to dash away.

“Lyssa, have you not forgotten something?” Angelina called.

The girl ducked her head and walked back to Alef. “Thank you, uncle, and may the One God protect you when you fly.” He nodded, and she raced off.

Troy felt a lump in his throat as he watched. ‘Ah, Family!’ he thought, not for the first time since arriving on Earth, ‘what a wonderful thing to have in your life.’

They all moved on to a great hall. Troy’s attention was drawn to the array of photographs hanging on the walls. “These are our teachers and mentors past and present,” Angelina told the group proudly. “Each of them have contributed to who we and our students have become.”

One photo particularly caught Troy’s eye. He called Brad over, pointed at the picture, and said, “Does this lady look familiar to you?”

“Could it be her?” Brad replied in awe after scrutinizing the photo. “Angelina, do you have other photos of this lady? What’s her story?”

Angelina looked at the two men sadly, then she turned to Alef to ask him to continue leading the others in a tour of the trades school. “You two come into my office,” she demanded briskly of Troy and Brad.

“I feel as though I have been summoned to the principal’s office for some misdemeanor,” Troy commented. Angelina turned to glare at him then gave him a weak smile and hurried on.

“How do you think you know that lady?” she demanded, once they had been seated. Troy told her about meeting Mrs. Grenville in Vancouver before they left for this trip.

“Esther Gates came to us through the United Church of Canada’s outreach program, Health Through Literacy, that was just in its infancy at the time. She was a wonderful elementary school teacher and a very good friend,” Angelina said.

“Was? What happened to her?” Troy asked.

“Esther and I had corresponded for some years; she and her husband were regular donors to our project. She believed in what we were trying to accomplish for underprivileged girls, as did several others at the Naramata School where she taught. After her husband died and their son was settled at University in Vancouver, Esther felt at loose ends, so I talked her into coming here to join us. Esther worked with us for five years before she became ill, and we all felt it would be better for her to return to Canada. We were told her flight arrived safely in Canada, but the air shuttle from Vancouver to the Okanagan valley crash-landed in a nearby lake.”

“Well, Angelina, we may have good news for you. If the lady we met is Esther, she is indeed alive but suffers from amnesia. Do you have other photos of her? You said her married name was Gates. Could she have remarried? Does the name Grenville sound at all familiar? They have a vineyard in the Okanagan. Her son, the one we met, is an astronomer with the planetarium in Vancouver," Brad told her.

"She said it was my use of the phrase, 'The One God,' that tweaked a memory, and she spoke and understood our native language," Troy added.

"Oh my, yes, that must have been Esther," Angelina said optimistically. "She loved the Dogon history and made a point of learning our language. I don't know about her son but she herself had a great interest in astronomy. Yes, it must have been our Esther you met. Oh, how wonderful! Do you have an address or contact information for her?"

Brad said, "No, just a phone number for her son. But we promised to meet with her on our way back. Her son will arrange it as soon as we know when we will be arriving in Vancouver. Would you like to write to Esther? We could deliver a letter for you."

"Oh, yes, I would like that very much! Thank you," she said, with an uncharacteristically large smile.

The conference with Syvers and the Commander-in-Chief went well, Troy thought. Though his uncle had not made any decisions yet, he seemed to favor Maria's staying here, and he was amenable to Troy's suggestion that Raj remain in this area to continue his part of the Earth mission. Uncle Ben seemed genuinely relieved to hear that the lady they had met in Vancouver was probably the Esther who had taught school on Dogon land years before, and he had urged Troy to return to Canada as soon as they could do so. 'Yes, it went well,' Troy thought, 'thanks be to the One God.'

Chapter 24

Seated in their private cabin, on the jumbo-jet they had boarded in Frankfurt, Germany, heading for Canada, all three men were tired and a little cranky. Ted had been told to accompany Troy and Brad to Canada to work with them there, while Raj settled in Mali. Troy wasn't sure why Ted had been required to come along, but he trusted that Syvers had his reasons, and Ted's expertise would be an asset on their next mission.

"I really wish we could have used our launch craft for this trip. It would have been so much faster!" Brad lamented once again. "I mean, why sit for 27 hours in this antiquated airplane after three tedious stop-overs, when it could have been a few hours' flight at most?"

"This is one of the more modern machines for its time," Ted reminded him. "You are just bored by all this inaction, Brad. Don't blame that on Earth's lack of technology. Humans made great strides in understanding aerodynamics in their 20th century, you must agree."

Troy sat in silence, ignoring their bickering, rethinking all that had occurred of late. The time he had spent with the Dogon priest yesterday had been both enjoyable and enlightening - illuminating so many things about his own people on Fentanys and about human evolution here on Earth. Troy had purchased a small, carved wooden quistyr encased in a tooled goatskin sheath that the monks made and sold to tourists. Troy planned to give it to Jimmy with Nancy's permission. It was a pleasure seeing Maria so genuinely happy to be able to stay on Earth, in what she believed was her new role now.

And Raj, too, was so much more relaxed and content since he had been granted leave to work in Mali, pending the Intergalactic Counsel's ruling regarding his 'indiscreet behavior' on Earth.

Troy's call to Esther's son had confirmed for Angelina, much to her delight, that Esther was indeed the lady who had worked with her years ago. As well, Uncle Ben had confirmed that he and Troy's father would be back in Earth's orbit within the month. Yes, all had gone well, Troy thought, as he leaned back with his hands behind his head.

Vancouver's weather was dull, grey, and overcast when the men arrived in the early morning. They quickly booked into the hotel the travel agent had arranged for them. They decided that they would order a light breakfast and just decompress. Later, Troy called Kevin; Ted had specifically wanted to meet him and Fritz, and to visit the university science facilities. The next morning Troy would be meeting with Esther as prearranged.

Meeting with Esther, now that he knew her identity, was a genuine pleasure. She read Angelina's letter, and with tears of happiness, she asked, "How is Angelina? Is she well? Tell me about the school. We, at Naramata, had heard there to be some expansions, but please tell me all." Esther laughed at his description of Angelina's driving and had been thrilled to hear about the school. "Alef did obtain his pilot's license. Isn't that wonderful? He always was an ambitious young man."

"And what took you to Mali, Troy? It is an unusual travel destination unless you have an interest in the Dogon," Esther asked coyly.

Troy, following their back-story, explained Maria's part in the Xernex mission - evaluation of the effect of pollution on the land, and how he and Brad had decided to meet her there while holidaying in Africa.

"But Troy, you have a connection with the Dogon too, do you not?"

"Yes," Troy replied smoothly, "I find them and their culture very fascinating, and the concept that humankind may have encountered more intelligent off-Earth beings in the distant past. Well, it makes a kind of sense doesn't it, Esther?" Troy ventured to add.

She studied him for a moment then just nodded. "So where are you and Brad off to next?" she asked.

Troy told her they were going to evaluate the huge garbage pools in the Pacific Ocean and also take a brief foray into the Arctic. Then he asked her to say hello to Angelina from him the next time she wrote to her, said his goodbyes, and left.

Kevin was happy to hear from Troy and was amenable to having them come by for another tour. "Is there any area in particular that your new crew member wanted to see?" he asked.

"I'm not sure, Kevin," Troy replied truthfully. "Ted was assigned to us only recently and comes with a lot of expertise that will be of benefit to our mission but what, other than genuine curiosity, he may be looking for, I don't know."

"Oh well, we will see as we go. I'll check our schedule and chat with Fritz then get back to you, Ok?"

"That will be fine. Thank you, Kevin."

During the visit to the Vancouver Aquarium and the University Science Center, Ted mostly just observed, asked some questions, but made very few comments. Brad, on the other hand, was excited to hear about the Biology Department's analysis and comments on the specimens he had brought from the garbage pools in the 'Bermuda Triangle.'

"These specimens and your description of the area have convinced the Board of Directors to allow us to mount an expedition to the Pacific garbage pools early next year," said Barbara, one of the Department heads. She was clearly thrilled to be part of the mission.

"Wow, that's great," Brad said. "We are heading in that direction ourselves shortly. We could coordinate our trips and compare our findings."

Fritz, overhearing this comment, could not resist bugging Troy again about allowing them to utilize the Xernex submersible for this exploration.

"You just don't give up Fritz, do you," Troy replied with a laugh.

"No, I don't, and be warned, young man, I usually get what I want."

"I don't doubt it," Troy muttered under his breath. Fritz just grinned and carried on with the tour.

That evening, Ted contacted Syvers then suggested Troy chat with his uncle telepathically if he could. Troy was puzzled but excused himself to go into his bedroom to try and contact Ben. Ben, it seemed, had been waiting for his contact.

"Troy! How are you, my nephew?" Ben greeted heartily.

"We are all doing well. Ted suggested we chat, you and me. Is everything okay there? Is my father well?"

"Oh, I did not mean to frighten you when I suggested this means of communicating! Your father is malnourished and fatigued but fine. We have docked the Triton in the Xernex, and we are on our way to Earth's orbit. There is much though that you and I need to discuss, Troy."

"Okay, I am glad father is getting well. So, what is it that I need to know, Uncle Ben?"

Ben went on to explain that in view of what had happened to Ches and with the mission to Earth, he went to the Intergalactic Council for guidance. Several changes were going to be made as a result. Ted had been sent along with Brad and Troy as an observer to confirm what had been reported. "This is not in any way a negative reflection on you or Brad, Troy," his uncle assured him. "Ted has had extensive military training in orienteering and reconnaissance, and we need him to assess certain situations with a new perspective."

"Yes, I can see the point of that," Troy agreed.

"There will be several changes made immediately," Ben went on to explain. "Maria, as agreed, will be allowed to remain on Earth. Raj is to complete this Earth mission as agreed, but he will be banned from further intergalactic missions. He may return to Fentanys in a civilian capacity or remain on earth with no further contact with Sirius, just like Maria. The choice is his. You will be asked to return to the Xernex to supervise the repairs of your father's ship, Troy. You are, after all, an architect, and we need your expertise in that capacity. But right now, you and Brad, with Ted's assistance, are to complete your Earth mission as planned. Hopefully, it can be completed within the next six Earth months. As well, you have been given permission to work with this Fritz fellow at the Science Center. With his marine architects and engineers, you can help them to develop a replica, but not an exact duplicate, of the submersible you developed for us. Ted will arrange the details for this, and he will know which technologies to share and which to keep secret. Are you comfortable with that, Troy?"

"That is a lot to think about, Uncle Ben, and I am sure I will have more questions once I think it through. So, we are to evacuate from Earth within six months?"

"Yes."

"I think that can be accomplished, and uncle, thank you. I look forward to seeing you all again. Say hello to father for me."

"Will do, the One God go with you, Troy. We will chat again soon."

Troy sat in silence for a few moments before returning to where Ted and Brad were waiting for him.

"How much of all this were you aware of Ted?" Troy asked abruptly.

"Only classified information, and hey, don't shoot the messenger, okay?" Ted said, flinging up his arms in a submissive stance.

Troy glared at him for a moment then smirked and said, "You are forgiven. So, what does Brad know?"

"That is up to you, captain," Ted said with a smart salute.

Brad took all the news with his usual nonchalance, asked a few questions, then suggested that they all get some sleep.

The next day, the men were at the science center again so Troy could inform them of Xernex's decision to allow Fritz's marine architect to help develop a similar, though not exact replica, of the Xernex submersible. As well, he told Kevin and Fritz they would be allowed to mount a joint expedition to the Pacific, though not, as Fritz had hoped, to the South China Sea. "Our advisers feel that the area is too precarious politically for us to be involved," Troy had asserted. Fritz was thrilled at the prospect, so Troy left it to Ted to work out the details of this project with Fritz and Kevin. There would be some exchange of information and financial arrangements involved that Troy would rather not have had to deal with anyway.

The next day, Troy called Maria and told her the Intergalactic Council's decision to allow her to remain on earth. She was thrilled! ''But you understand, do you not, that this means no more contact with Sirius or Fentanys," Troy warned her.

"Yes, I know, Troy. This is what I need to do and want to do."

"Then may the One God be with you," he said then asked that she call Raj if he was available.

Raj had been expecting Troy's call. "That is a fair judgement," he agreed. "Thank you, Troy, for intervening on my behalf. I will let you know soon what my plans are in that regard. Meanwhile, I have already started pulling together a team to continue work here in the Mali desert. Hopefully, I will be able to complete my mission mandate within the allotted time frame."

"Good, keep me posted."

"Will do, captain," Raj replied.

***

Several days later, back in Desolation Sound, the men checked the launch craft and submersible in preparation for their trip to the arctic. Their agreement with Fritz was that the three men would use the launch craft to join up with the university oceanography team at specified coordinates in the Pacific Ocean. Then, as a joint effort, they would use the submersible to help explore the garbage pools there. This would aid their research and give their engineers working experience on the sub under Troy's tutoring. Of course, they would be sharing any new data found at the site. As Fritz's team was aiming to launch their exploration early in the coming year, it seemed sensible for Troy, Brad, and Ted to make their trip to the Arctic Ocean early in December. They had been warned that they may encounter severely frigid conditions, but Troy was confident their craft would withstand the rigors of the northern climate.

"Well, the equipment seems in order," Brad pointed out, "so how do we proceed? What's the plan, captain?"

"Ted?" Troy asked.

"Uh, what I haven't told you, and what Troy suspects, is that the Intergalactic Council has additional conditions for this trip." Troy nodded, and Ted continued. "Besides checking for signs of pollution in the northern regions, we are to take measurement of the intensity of the sun's rays reaching Earth through the north portal and to search for sources of pyrolusite."

Brad immediately objected, saying, "I can see the reason for checking the intensity of the sun's rays in view of the expanding breakdown of the ozone layer, but I thought we were to observe only. Mining for, or even purchasing, quantities of a native Earth metal cannot be construed as observation. What can the council be thinking?"

"I can't divine their thoughts," Ted said with a shrug, "but, Brad, you know as well as I do that Fentanys is quickly depleting its own resources of that metal, so either new sources must be found, or alternatives need to be developed."

"True," Brad conceded, "but that mandate feels more like an imposition that an observation."

The men sat in silence thinking on this for a few moments, then Troy turned to Ted and said, "The Arctic is a vast region. Do we have any guidance as to where to start looking?"

"Yes, the Earth specialists suggested we set down on Meighan Island in the Canadian Arctic Archipelago. It is a small, mainly uninhabited island in open water near the Geographical North Pole, but far enough from it so as not to be hampered by the magnetic disturbance that affects air travel near the pole," answered Ted.

"Okay, that seems workable," Troy agreed, after checking the area maps and relevant coordinates; they went on to discuss further logistics regarding travel and work in frigid conditions.

"We will need to make a shopping trip to Powell River to get warmer outerwear before we leave. How long do you think we will be in the Arctic?" Brad asked.

"A few weeks at most, I hope," Ted replied. "That will bring us back here before the Christmas season. Kevin's family has invited us to celebrate this special holiday with them, remember. I'm curious about this Christian celebration."

"Yes, so am I," Brad agreed. "After seeing how the Dogan maintained the spiritual roots of their origins, it will be interesting to compare the similarities and differences between their spiritual evolvement and those of other cultures."

"I believe that one of the Christian Christmas rites involves the giving and receiving of gifts, just as the Dogon do at certain celebrations," Cee observed.

"Oh yes, and there is the belief that a grandfatherly figure named Santa brings gifts from the North Pole to good boys and girls," Troy added. "Maybe we will meet Santa on our trip. Jimmy would love that!"

"We will have to take a photo of ourselves with Santa as proof that he really exists," Brad teased.

***

On a balmy evening in early March, Kevin and Rachael sat on the deck at their cabin on Savary Island. The sun was sinking low on the western horizon, and the warm breeze was laden with the scent of the magnolia in bloom. Kevin leaned back, resting his head on the back of the deckchair, and just breathed in the warm moist scented air, grateful as he always was, to be here with family.

"Jimmy was so disappointed not to have been able to say goodbye to Cee," Rachael commented. "But looking at the three of them now standing on the dock together; I'm happy to see Eric and Nancy happy together again."

"Yes, that is nice to see, and Troy had a hand in their reunion," Kevin said.

Rachael turned to her husband and raised an eyebrow.

"Oh, you missed that, did you dear? Troy caught up with Eric at the Christmas Party and told him exactly what he thought of a man who could treat such a beautiful family so carelessly." Kevin chuckled. "Oh Rachael, you would have enjoyed watching that exchange. Troy is calm and methodical, which makes him a good leader, but despite Eric's extensive military training, Troy had Eric cowed that night!"

"I'm sure that Jimmy's delight at receiving that quistyr was a rub as well. Look! He is still wearing it everywhere he can. Oh, and Nancy thinks she may be expecting another child," Rachael added.

"Good heavens, how do you women know these things so soon?"

"Woman's intuition, dear," Rachael replied smugly.

"Mommy, look," Jimmy squealed, pointing up to the northern sky. Rachael and Kevin rushed over to the side of the deck for a better look and called for the rest of the family to come.

A flash of brilliant light raced across the sky, seeming to come right at them, then it veered sharply to the left and rose high to disappear in the west behind the setting sun.

"Showoffs," John muttered under his breath and chuckled.

"Hot chocolate in the den," Rachael called.

"With marshmallows? Colored ones, Auntie Rachael?" Jimmy yelled, and he raced back up the dock.

"Cee isn't coming back, is he, Grampa?" Jimmy asked later, breaking the silence that had fallen as everyone settled in the den.

"No, Jimmy," Wayne replied quietly, "Cee, Troy, and Brad must go somewhere else, on another mission."

"But we could visit them, or they could visit us, couldn't they?" Jimmy persisted.

"No, son, where they go is too far away for us to follow," Eric replied as he lifted Jimmy onto his knees. "But we can remember them and be grateful to have met them, right?"

"Yes," Kevin added, "and did you know, Jimmy, that there is a school in a faraway place called Mali in Africa. The school there does not have all the wonderful supplies, books, and desks, or even baseballs and bats, like your school has. When Troy heard about the schools' needs, he took all the money that our university paid him to help make a new submersible, and he donated it to that school so other boys and girls in that other faraway land could have the same advantages as you do."

"Did Troy really give away all that money to the school, Dad?" Keira asked in awe. "What a wonderful contribution to furthering literacy around the world!"

"Yes, he did that, honey. Also, their contribution of time and shared knowledge with our science department have been a significant help. We still have a long way to go on the issue of Earth's pollution problem, but we are making headway, thanks in part to having met those fine men."

"Having read about the Dogon history," Rachael mused, "well I wondered..."

“We will never know, honey,” Kevin asserted. “Perhaps they were sojourners here, meant to stay only a while, then move on to share with others along the way.”

Ode to Earth

By Etroygylus

Silvery white, shining bright, the most beautiful and beloved of planets in your galaxy
We orbit closer; even more stunning as we draw nearer
Fluffy white clouds partly obscure azure waters, lush green forests, broad pockets of land
We dodge space stations, derelict satellites, and debris
Splash-down!
Embraced now in the cool, undulating, saline waters; in the silence, we are cradled in your loving womb
Thank you, Mother Earth!
Your flora and fauna, recognizing our unique energetic imprint, welcome us
We explore, study, and learn about this legendary place, verifying what we already know and learning so much more
You, dear Earth, do not disappoint!
Intermingling with human inhabitants is a challenge on this mission of peace and discovery
They do not recognize our presence as other than themselves, and we work well under this guise
Human beings intrigue us!

Our research verifies that Earth's humans have a great capacity for caring and sharing; they are strong physically and mentally, and they are creative and innovative

We are gratified to watch the love displayed within the family unit, between spouses, and within the small communities

This warms the soul!

For so long, our home planet has been a wasteland - colorless, depleted

To recoup, we watch and learn, hungrily absorbing what is here on earth, hoping to emulate this warmth back home

But then... the newscasts... could these reports be true?

Wars and rumors of wars, massive pollution of oceans and land, wanton over-use of natural resources, exploitation of the poor and under-privileged, ethnic cleansing, child exploitation, abuse

Why?

Where is the brotherly love, the respect and caring for self and others, the respect and love for your wonderous home planet

We weep!

Earthlings, without love and care, all becomes a wasteland

Humans, your Mother Earth's provisions will sustain all, but if you persist in your disrespectful selfishness, disregarding the consequences of your present action, she cannot continue to provide.

Beware desolation!

We will not interfere; you must decide!

We shall return!

About the Author

Marguerite Antonio has spent much of her life helping others as a spiritual healer and Reiki Master. She has an instinctive affinity to the aquatic, particularly the dolphin. Her deep connection to Mother Earth is evident both in Ancion and this latest novel Sojourner. Marguerite has written and published other books as well, a textbook on Reiki, a compilation of short stories, and an historical novel.

After years of living near her beloved ocean she chose to reside in Edmonton, Alberta to be near friends and family. Her passion for our planet continues to inspire her writing.

www.ingramcontent.com/pod-product-compliance
Lightning Source LLC
LaVergne TN
LVHW091132080826
845145LV00008B/2129

* 9 7 8 1 7 7 3 5 4 4 6 1 8 *